# The Unbreakable Triple Dare

# The Unbreakable Triple Dare

Philip Burns

First Published 2010



Published by Completely Novel

ISBN 978-1-84914-057-7

*For a special class that inspired me to write this*

*&*

*Sian who helped me to finish it!*

# Contents

# Chapter 1 - Mr Jones

Mr Jones, the school caretaker, was a kind elderly man who had worked at the school for 25 years. All the children loved Mr Jones and saw him as a second grandfather with his silver grey hair, neatly cut beard and small round spectacles perched on the end of his nose. However, drop some litter or make a mess in the corridor while Mr Jones was around and you could end up on 'Litter Picking Duty' during lunch and break times wearing a bright high-visibility jacket, so the whole school would know what you had done.

Darkness had fallen upon the silent school where Mr Jones worked. Books lay dormant on desks and pencils stood to attention in brightly coloured pots, awaiting the next day's work. The floors along the long winding empty corridor shimmered from the moonlight cascading from the skylights above. Other corridor walls disappeared into the darkness covered from floor to ceiling with football and netball display boards showing match fixtures and team photos; locked display cabinets protecting the Spend-A-

Penny League Winner's Cup and Runners-up shield for the District Sports Competition. The weary children had left many hours earlier followed swiftly by their teachers clutching their heavy bags as they shuffled towards their cars. Without children or teachers the school was now an abandoned building left dormant, sleeping, readying itself for the next day of hustle and bustle.

Mr Jones would usually check carefully that the school was properly locked up after the cleaners had finished but tonight was different. He wanted to attend his Granddaughter's birthday party as he had never missed one since she was born, 8 years ago. Earlier that day he had asked the headteacher's permission to leave the classrooms unlocked, just until he returned from the party, and had planned to lock all the external doors. St Mark's Primary School was located in a very small village at the end of a winding country lane. Unless you attended or worked at the school you were unlikely to know of its existence. Even the postman had trouble some days! In the 25 years that Mr Jones had been caretaker there hadn't been any security issues at the school and he thought tonight wasn't going to be any different!

The headteacher had agreed to Mr Jones' request so he finished his duties earlier than usual and, knowing he wouldn't miss Dawn's party, cheerfully locked the front doors assuming the school was empty.

However, as the echoes of the caretaker's footsteps slowly faded down the long silent corridor, a sound could be heard coming from class 6! The silent still air was shattered by a crash of books tumbling down followed by a loud high-pitched scream.

As a dare, two children had hidden themselves in the class 6 cupboard, knowing that their teacher had left promptly at 3.15pm to get ready for the PTA Quiz Night. This was not your usual playground dare, as earlier that day, an 'Unbreakable Triple Dare' had been made, which meant that those who had accepted this dare had to stay in the cold dark school *all* night.

Slowly the cupboard door opened and out stepped Jamie, the first of the hideaways.

‘Oww my ears! Didn't I tell you not to touch that book?’

‘It wasn't my fault,’ Sophie said rubbing her head, where a hard heavy book had just recently hit her. ‘If you’d moved over when I’d asked you to, then I wouldn't have needed to move the book that was digging into my neck. How was I to know it was supporting the five books above it.’

‘Well, if you hadn't found my dare so funny, Holly wouldn’t have dared you to stay with me and then you wouldn't have been hit on the head!’ Jamie left Sophie rubbing her head and began to look for a way to the classroom door.

Whilst searching  he cast his mind back over the events of the last two days, wondering why he had agreed to the dare which had brought him there.

# Chapter 2 - Hugh

**Wednesday: Two Days Ago**

The bell was rung loudly by the over-enthusiastic lunchtime bell Monitor, Emma-Lee, who thought for at least a few minutes she was in charge of the school. Classes wouldn't stop and lunch wouldn't begin without her ring of the bell and she was in full command of it all!

The bell was the signal of the amazing transformation from normal primary school to African safari. The children, like animals at feeding time, stampeded along the corridors. Gaggles of geese stopped to chat in the middle of the corridors and the park rangers tried to keep control of the ravenous animals, issuing commands like 'Walk! Don't run!' and 'No pushing!'

Just like the rest of the school, it was your usual lunch time chaos in class 6. The boys had rushed from the classroom to get the best seat in the hall, with some being called back to push their chairs in properly. The girls, on the other hand, knew that it didn't matter which table you were on. Sally's mum, who was mid-day supervisor today, would let the girls go up and get their school lunches first anyway. So they were loitering in the cloakroom, standing in front of the small mirrors checking that their hair still looked perfect and that their lip gloss didn't need topping up, chatting about which boys they liked or who had seen the new clothing range in New Look.

Every child in class 6 had their usual table to sit at with hardly anyone deciding to change or swap places. At the far end of the row of tables sat the 'Time Travellers'. These were the boys that would constantly talk about Star Wars or who the best Dr Who was and usually had the same Lego lunch box as each other. No girls would ever be seen on their table and they were usually the last to leave after debating how best to defeat Colonel Vogel at the end of the Desert Ambush level of the 'Lego Indiana Jones' computer game. Should they destroy the trucks before attacking Vogel? Or land a few punches, destroy the trucks and then go back to finish off Vogel?

Next to them were the 'Flower girls' who are all members of the Gardening Club, Eco-Warrior Club and are dedicated Playground Pals. The topic of conversation at one end of the table was which animal they thought was the cutest, bunnies or kittens. While at the other end they were discussing how they could get the caretaker to extend their vegetable patch, as it was far too small to grow marrows.

On the third table, which was a 'by invite only' table, were the 'Girly Girls'. Hot topic of conversation this lunch time was where Alfie should be *told* to take Holly on their first date, with the cinema or bowling being the top two choices. They also chatted about what they most liked in the Summer New Look collection, whether it was the studded skinny white denim stretch fit jeans or the beautiful lace and butterfly printed vest top with the scoop neckline with racer back. And all of this while dunking the rock hard cakes cook usually made into their cup of water!

Finally you had the 'Boot Boys', the members of the school football A team. Arsenal had just beaten Chelsea 3-1 in last night's Cup Final and there was a huge debate as to whether Theo Walcott was tripped brutally or dramatically dived entering the penalty area.

Jamie sat on the 'Boot Boys' table and, like a few of the others on his table, had quickly scoffed his entire packed lunch to ensure that he got out onto the field first.

After Sally's mum had made him pick up the crisps he and the others had been throwing at each other, he quickly jogged (as no running was allowed in school) out of the hall into the long corridor. Expertly throwing his lunch box onto the shelf without slowing down, he walked quickly through the classroom, ensuring that Miss Chalk wasn't secretly hiding in her cupboard trying to catch any pupils running, and then he was freed! He thought each day, that it was like escaping from prison, but he knew in a hour the guards would be out rounding them all up again for the next session of hard labour with pens and pencils!

While Jamie still had his freedom he was going to make the most of it and he did what his friends did every lunch time, he visited Hugh. You could trust Hugh with anything, even who you fancied and the secret would remain forever untold. You see, Hugh wasn't your normal playground friend, he wasn't actually a person, *he* was a large fifty year old oak tree! Hugh was very special to them.

It was during their first lunchtime, when they had just started class 6; they had decided to adopt the tree on the far side of the large playing field as their place to hang out.

In previous years, children in year 6 would hang out by 'Stumpy'. A large tree had been cut down many years ago due to hurricane-force winds damaging it in 1990, leaving a large tree stump sticking out of the ground. Teachers used it for Science and Geography lessons, counting the rings and seeing how old it was but at lunchtime it was commandeered for class 6 business. That was until the new Activity Trail was installed over the tree stump during the summer break; Stumpy was no more!

But now they had Hugh, who was just far enough away that the mid-day supervisors couldn't see clearly what was going on by the tree. So as long as they weren't fighting or seen going out-of-bounds they wouldn't be bothered by the busy lunchtime staff. This made it the perfect place for dares!

Jamie was the first to reach Hugh and turned around quickly to gloat at who he had beaten. He was one of the fastest in the class and always came first at sports day. On this occasion it was Max who came in second place. Even though exhausted from their run they did their customary hand shake which started with a normal handshake, then into a thumb grasp followed by a quick backhand front hand slap, linking into the finger touching wiggle and finishing off with an attitude click to the side.

Jamie was a typical boy and would never be seen with his shirt tucked in. He had short dark spikey hair that had taken him at least half-an-hour that morning to get just right, ensuring that a hair wasn't out of place. Jamie had a few freckles on his button nose and when he smiled had dimples on his cheeks. He was really embarrassed by these as the girls always told him how cute they were! Girlfriends were not on Jamie's agenda, as he wanted to be a professional football player. All the girls he knew just got in the way of a football game or would end up kicking him on the shins, instead of the ball. However, he did have friends that were girls and when he wasn't playing football he would hang out with them by Hugh.

Max, the second fastest in the class, was Jamie's best friend and was only slightly older than him. Jamie had only just reached double digits with his birthday last week and Max was the first on his invite list for the party. Max had known Jamie since Reception and his parents were very good friends with Jamie's; he even called Jamie's mum and dad, Uncle and Aunty they were that close! Max didn't like short hair and, much to his mum's annoyance, kept his light brown hair long with a side-sweep fringe covering the face. He was shorter than Jamie but made up for it by being stronger which was always useful being the school's central defender and putting in strong tackles. They had many adventures growing up and were always out playing after school.

Only last week Jamie and Max were out on their bikes riding along a dried up river bed when Max thought it would be a good idea to try and jump his bike across from one side to the other. He had found a good spot where the bank was raised on one side with a path leading up the hill which would give him a good run up. Jamie had decided that the jump was too far and he would never be crazy enough to try it.

Just as he was going to express he fears to Max he noticed he was already at the top of the path readying himself for the upcoming jump. Jamie called out to Max but it was too late. Max was off and gaining speed as he pumped his peddles as fast as they would go. He hit the ramp perfectly and soared into the air, crouching his body to make it as streamlined as possible. The air had blown his fringe off his face which was now flowing freely behind his head. Not wearing a safety helmet was going to be something he was going to regret in about ten seconds.

He began to lose height and the other side of the river bank appeared too far to reach. As if in slow motion, his front wheel embedded itself into the bank like a javelin, throwing the back wheel into the air and forward. Max was catapulted over the handle bars like a stuntman falling out of a window, legs and arms flailing in all directions. Instinct took over from reasonable thought and his arms were soon clutching and protecting his head, as he summersaulted, then landed in the tangle of weeds and stinging nettles. Jamie winced imagining Max's pain. Luckily Max didn't break any bones but had a very sore face and a body covered with many painful stings that a mountain of dock leaves wasn't going to help relieve. What made Jamie laugh next was that Max stood up and asked 'Does that count as making it over?'

'Do you know who else is coming?' asked Max, after finishing their greeting ritual.

'Well I heard that Alfie was coming, which means Holly will be here...'

'What?' replied Max, spinning his head around, mouth wide open in shock. 'I know Alfie secretly fancies Holly but doesn't she realise that we dared him to ask her out?'

'No and she didn't believe me when I told her it was just a dare! But you know what girls are like?' Jamie rolled his eyes and shook his head while Max nodded in agreement. 'You tell them one thing and they think that *you* want them to think that, but actually think the thing that you don't want them to think. Got it?'

Max looked perplexed; he was never clever enough to get into the top groups but copied enough from Jamie to stay in the middle group. Trying to sound like he knew what Jamie was talking about Max replied, 'Yeah of course I do, that's what girls are like!'

'What *are* girls like?' said Kate turning up out of the blue, swinging her long light brown hair from her eyes and looking intently at Max.

Caught off guard, Max and Jamie tried in vain to make something up about not being as quick as boys, but it didn't convince Kate at all! She lifted her left eye brow and shook her head, whilst shooting a very disapproving look towards both boys. Then, without a word, she went to sit in the shade Hugh was casting on the recently cut grass.

'I've told Sophie and Holly that as soon as they've eaten they should meet us here. Do you know who else is coming?'

'Well as I was just telling Max, Alfie's coming and...'

'Oh my God, I'm so glad I invited Holly then. You do know that Alfie asked her out on Monday and she told Sophie to tell you, to tell Alfie that she would think about it?' Without even stopping to hear their answer, Kate continued at pace to tell a minute by minute account of every little detail that had happened during Monday's lunchtime, unaware that both Max and Jamie already knew. Kate could easily tell you every piece of gossip at the school and even what the teachers were up to in the staff room. If you wanted to know something, Kate was the girl to ask. How much of it was based on the truth no-one ever knew, as you never got to ask any questions once she got going.

Just as the boys were losing the will to live and looking likely that they were going to fall asleep at any minute, they could see hope and rescue running towards them, in the form of Alfie.

Alfie was the third musketeer of the boys group and would always be there to back them up. He was the St Mark's football team striker and was one goal behind Jamie in getting the Golden Boot for lead goal scorer. He wasn't your typical striker as he carried a bit of weight and was quite chubby; to his friends he was known as 'Hamster'.

He earned this nickname at the Christmas party when he was challenged to a marshmallow eating contest called 'Chubby Bunnies' where, after each marshmallow, you have to say 'Chubby Bunnies' and if you couldn't you were out. After eight marshmallows only Alfie and Greig Browning (last year's champion) were left standing. Holly had reached the top three but eight was one-too-many and she had to spit out the half melted marshmallows onto the floor and, to Jamie's disgust, his shoes.

The ninth marshmallow was squashed and squeezed into his already over-crowded mouth. Alfie's cheeks were bulging but holding, all he had to do was say two words. Greig had just had his turn and managed to say Chubby before his mouth's contents exploded, covering poor unfortunate Rachel who happened to be passing by. It was up to Alfie now and all eyes were on him, could he say 'Chubby Bunnies' and be crowned the champion?

'Chub...' As Alfie opened his mouth a marshmallow tried to escape but he caught it and pushed it back in. 'Chubby......' He was on the verge of gagging and failure. '....Bunnies!' Alfie had done it and the whole class erupted into cheers and clapping. However, slapping him on the back was not the best move for Jamie to make, as this led another marshmallow mess on the floor.

From the cheers someone had called Alfie 'Hamster Boy' and the class picked up on this and started chanting

‘Hamster! Hamster!’ and this name had stuck with him ever since.

Alfie’s weight didn’t bother him in the slightest, as there was nothing he couldn’t do with a football. If there was, it wasn’t worth knowing. He was like a ballerina when he had the ball, pirouetting around players and demonstrating a lovely port de bras when shooting at goal, although no-one would make that comparison to his face! He knew every Brazilian trick in the book from the ‘Ronaldo Chop’ to the ‘Robinho Stepover’ and when he got going there was no stopping him with his quick pace.

‘Hi ya!’ said Alfie suddenly spotting a tennis ball underneath the nearest bush and darting over to retrieve it.

‘Alright Hamster!’ replied Jamie while Max joined Alfie in retrieving the ball, holding back a very prickly branch with his foot so as not to get punctured himself. After freeing the ball both boys returned to the tree where Kate and Jamie were sitting and started passing the ball between each other.

'So, what were you talking to Jamie and Max about Kate?' asked Alfie, making a low pass to Max who completely ignored the ball, returning it to its hiding place beneath the bush, never to be seen again. Looking up at Max, wondering why his friend had missed the pass, he saw a look of disbelief on his friend's face and body language that yelled out at him 'We just about managed to survive one re-telling!' He then instantly regretted asking Kate the question.

Kate was oblivious to the exchange of body language and turning to face Alfie decided to tell the whole story again right from the beginning, ignoring the moans from those who had just heard it.

To the boys great delight, Kate arrived quickly at the end of her enthusiastic re-telling of the gossip. '…and I was just saying that Holly really likes you and she is still thinking about your question.'

Alfie had zoned out when he heard it was about the dare with Holly. He had already heard Jamie's commentary on what he said, the reply he got and wasn't really interested in a girl's viewpoint of the dare. That was until his brain suddenly switched onto the part where Holly really liked him and his hearing quickly became tuned into Kate's frequency, comprehending the last few words.

He looked quickly between Max and Jamie like a meerkat on the lookout and on seeing their sheepish faces, realised that they hadn't yet told Kate it was just a dare. Holly still thought he had asked her out and his well made plans were unravelling.

Alfie knew that asking Holly out as a Dare would be a good indicator as to whether Holly liked him or not. A bit like a trial run whereby if the answer was no he could say 'Well it was just a dare!' and not get totally embarrassed by being rejected. However, even if the answer was yes he was still going to say it was a dare, as he still had the 'Inter School Cup Final' to play in and he couldn't have any distractions to achieve his goal, and that included girls to! At least he would still have the answer he had been longing for.

He had been working so hard during the season to make sure that St Mark's reached the final and would do anything to make sure they won. Any distraction could mean the difference between winning or losing the game. He had to tell Kate it was a dare.

'Kate, I think there is something I need to tell you.'

Max and Jamie felt they had let their best friend down by not telling the girls during morning play that it had just been a dare but the three whistles had signalled the end of play as they were about to. Max had even tried to pass a written note to Kate, on the back of his maths sheet, during lesson time but Miss Chalk had caught him. She had told him to stop passing the answers to Kate as she was quite capable of doing the work on her own.

Kate was not going to be happy with what Alfie was about to tell her and when she got angry with someone, everything she knew about them was used as ammunition to shoot them down. No-one stood a chance against her.

The boys thought Alfie was very brave to be walking into the firing line knowing the consequences. They had to quickly think of a way to give Alfie a stay of execution as the heavy artillery was running hastily towards them in the form of Holly and Sophie. It was going to be a blood bath and there was nothing they could do to stop it. Jamie put his face in his hands and that's when the idea came to him. Alfie, the 'Hamster', would live to tell another tale.

'Yeah he wants to tell you that you've got a black mark on your face.' said Jamie, interrupting the condemned prisoner's confession.

'Where?' asked Kate.

Jamie secretly licked his finger, rubbed it in the dirt next to him as he rose to his feet and pressed his dirty finger on the exact place he thought the mark should be. 'It's right there!' Cleverly, this left a dark smudge on her cheek that Kate would clearly be able to see. The idea had come to him when he placed his face in his hands and noticed how covered in dust and dirt they were.

Kate, looking somewhat taken aback that her perfect face was now marked in some way, decided to check her face and hair again in the mirror, having only checked it moments before lunch.

Alfie, unaware Sophie and Holly were close to reaching Hugh, tried again to tell the truth but Max and Jamie bundled him to the ground and pointed out the potential pitfalls of his plan.

Sophie and Holly quickly appeared, both slightly out of breath having run all the way from the hall, and sat themselves down, ignoring the bundle of boys next to them. The girls, noticing Kate had her mirror out, immediately tended to her hair, pulling out their hairbrushes in readiness for the complete make-over about to take place.

It wasn't long before the group reverted to their usual routine with boys trying to dig holes in the ground with short pieces of sticks while the girls tying Kate's hair into a messy bun, gossiped in hushed voices so the boys didn't over-hear them.

'So, as I was telling you in the hall, Hamster is one handsome boy!' whispered Holly glanced flirtatiously to where Alfie was sitting. 'I love the way he spikes the back of his hair and combs it flat over the front. I still can't believe he actually asked me out, tell me again Kate what Hamster said to you.'

'Oh it was sooo lovely. Hamster came up to me and wanted to speak to me privately about you. He said that he thought you had lovely blue eyes like the ocean and you smelt like a beautiful flower picked on a summer's day and could I ask you if you would go out with him.'

Kate turned to Sophie while Holly looked towards Alfie again with a glazed adoring look on her face; the one you get when you have a huge crush on a Pop Star.

'He didn't actually say it like that,' whispered Kate so that this time Holly couldn't hear. 'He said he liked her eyes and she smelt nice!' Both Kate and Sophie giggled understanding the part they would play in getting Alfie and Holly together.

Sophie was a closer friend to Kate than she was to Holly. She is and has been Kate's neighbour since she moved into the area and started at St Mark's, in year 3. She even had a crush on Kate's older brother, who is two years older than. That was until he kidnapped her Barbie one day and tied it to a tree, all because his evil Action Man needed a doll to experiment on!

Sophie was a very pretty girl and always had lots of boys asking her out and Kate would always be on the case to vet them all with plenty of questions, knowing already their past dating history in full and whether they would be good boyfriend material for Sophie. No-one to date had passed Kate's scrutinisation although one year 5 boy nearly had. Kate thought he was cute but, before telling Sophie, decided to go out with him herself. This nearly broke up their friendship until Kate told Sophie what a bad decision it was, as he always picked his nose and was scared of older girls!

Holly was still daydreaming and looking longingly at Alfie. Sophie decided she wasn't going to get much out of Holly and asked Kate about the lovely bracelet she was wearing. 'I made it myself. My mum bought me a brilliant kit that has lots of different stones and charms that you can thread onto string.'

Everybody liked Kate's mum and thought she was cool as she was always going to different festivals singing and dancing with her band ‘Acorn’, and meeting lots of famous people. Only last year she performed on the same stage as Blue Star (who Sophie had posters of all over her room!) Kate’s dad used to play the guitar in a band and that’s how her parents had got together. They were both performing at the Glastonbury Festival 15 years ago and dad had heard kate’s mum’s beautiful voice on stage and instantly fell in love with her. Kate’s mum wrote a song about it with her band and had sung it at their wedding, which everyone thought was so romantic.

Kate also enjoyed playing the guitar and was really good after many one-to-one tuition sessions with her very patient dad! She also had a lovely singing voice which must have come from Mum’s side of the family because if you ever heard Kate’s dad sing, you would have thought a cat was being strangled! At this year’s talent show she played her guitar and sung in front of the whole school. When she finished her rendition of Blue Star’s new song ‘Believe in Love’ everyone gave her a standing ovation, even the tough Year 5 teacher had a tear in his eye!

‘Do you think you could make me a bracelet?’ asked Sophie after trying on one of Kate’s lovely bracelets.

‘Oh yeah, definitely. I have these wonderful pink gem stones!’ said Kate excitedly as she went into the finer details of the bracelet she could make for Sophie.

# Chapter 3 - Double Dare

'Right who's up for the first dare? Get into a circle and we'll begin.' said Holly, in her usual role as dare maker, deciding that everyone was ready for her to begin. She hadn't wanted the position when they first started the dares but everyone else thought she was the perfect girl for it. She was a Pisces through and through, which meant she would always go out of her way to help others, being a sensitive and loyal friend. The class trusted her with all their secrets and if a dare was going to be made-up she could use her creative skills to come up with the best ones. Which she usually did!

The boys simply spun around, throwing their mud covered sticks behind them, and formed half of the circle. Alfie was at one end and Jamie at the other with Max sandwiched in between. As the boys looked across the circle they couldn't quite work out why the girls were having so much trouble with this simple instruction.

Sophie and Kate, now with a new hairstyle, turned around where they were, leaving a space for Holly to crawl into and sit between them. Sophie, who found herself on the end nearest to Alfie, immediately got up as Holly had filled the space, and quickly sat on the other side of Kate linking arms, making sure there wasn't enough room for anyone to sit. This had all been pre-arranged between Kate and Sophie, who thought it was within their power to play cupid between Holly and Alfie.

Holly noticed who she was now sitting next to and felt a shiver run down her spine and her heart rate started to beat to a quicker rhythm. She had wanted to sit next to Alfie but wasn't bold enough to do so. Alfie smiled across at Holly who smiled and nervously giggled in return. She then quickly turned away from Alfie, her face, covered by her blonde wavy hair was now turning a bright shade of red, which matched her red hair grip.

Kate and Sophie, now intensely whispering to each other and giggling, looked across to a now glowing Holly and gave her a suggestive wink and nod which indicated that she should get even closer to Alfie.

'So who will it be first?' asked Alfie looking just as embarrassed by the attention that everyone was giving them; even Max and Jamie had slowly twigged what was going on. He hoped a diversion would ease the awkward situation. 'Holly?'

Taking the hint that if they changed the subject they wouldn't be bothered anymore, Holly began in her role as dare maker. 'Right who wants the next…'

'How come you get to make up the dares?' interrupted Max, turning to face the others. 'Holly always gives the dares so she doesn't get one herself.'

For once Max was right and as all the other children began to think about when the last time she had taken a dare, it slowly dawned on them all that Holly hadn't had a dare in months. One by one they all looked at Holly, expecting her to attempt an explanation, but she didn't. Instead she brightly and enthusiastically exclaimed, 'Yes you are right! Ok what is it going to be?'

Dares ranged from asking someone out to telling a teacher they liked their tie. The more embarrassing the dare the likelier it was going to be a good one. Only last week Holly double-dared Max to walk around the entire school field with his shirt tucked in. This in itself would have been a big enough dare for Max, who always had his shirt hanging out and would often roll his shirt when asked to tuck it in or even opt to put his jumper on when going into assembly, even if there was a heat wave! However, he also had to pull his trousers up as far as they would go, like a Super Wedgy, and tuck his trousers into his socks. Holly called it being 'Geek-a-fied'.

Confusion set in for a while as no one was sure who should come up with the new dare; nobody apart from Holly had been put in this position before. But eventually a smile could be seen spreading across Max's face. 'Ok I've got a dare for you, it's a double dare! Are you up for it?'

The rules of the game were quite simple, however, the consequences for breaking them were usually far worse. There were three levels of dares. First there was the simple dare – not too embarrassing. This usually involved saying something to a teacher or doing a silly dance. Secondly, there was the double dare – even more embarrassing and this often included an element of danger. Finally, there was the unbreakable triple dare – the toughest of all the dares and one that carried the highest risk of embarrassment or danger; only one person had ever completed a dare like this and survived the punishment for getting caught. Karl Walker. He was a legend at the school, although I don't think the caretaker was too happy when his size 5 foot went right through class 4's roof after clambering up the drain pipe and walking across the ceiling!

'Yes, I'll take the double dare.' replied Holly. 'What is it Max?'

'You're to go into school and get your pink mobile phone out of your bag.' Holly raised her hand but before Holly could deny it being in her bag, Max continued. 'We all know you don't hand your phone into the office! You are to get your phone, bring it out onto the field and then call the school office pretending to be a newspaper journalist.'

'What happens if Mrs Jenkins, the secretary, recognises my voice, I won't get to complete my dare?'

'Don't worry about that, Paul and Sally are office monitors today and Mrs Jenkins has to take her dog out for a walk during lunchtime.' replied Kate looking smugly towards the group, reminding everyone that she knew everything that went on at the school!

Looking slightly more worried, understanding the trouble she could get into, Holly rose to her feet and ran off towards school.

'So do you think she'll go through with it?' asked Kate as soon as Holly was out of earshot.

'Of course she will!' replied Sophie. 'She hasn't ever let any of us down before. She's seen all of us do dares and I don't think she'd back out!'

The group continued to speculate how she would manage to get her phone out of her bag without any of the patrolling teachers seeing her, when they were interrupted by an annoying ringtone coming from behind them. They all turned around and saw a very confident long blonde haired girl posing with her pink mobile to her ear! ‘No worries!’

‘Did you have any problems getting it?’ enquired Kate.

‘No, but just as I pulled out my phone, who should turn up but Charles Graham!’

‘Nooooo! Did he grass on you?’ asked Sophie.

If anyone was going to tell a teacher it was Charles Graham, he was the biggest rat of the class.

‘Luckily I was able to drop the phone into my dress pocket and pull out my hair brush. He thought I was being my girly self again and didn’t bother to stop. So, now onto the next part of the dare!’

As Holly sat down, she glanced over her shoulder to see if the coast was clear of lunchtime supervisors and began to dial the school office number. All the others grouped closely around Holly, trying to get into a good position to listen in on the conversation.

It wasn't long before a young boy answered the phone in a very posh voice, 'Good afternoon St Mark's Primary School. How may I help you?'

Holly giggled at hearing Paul put on such a posh telephone voice but managed to keep it under control and covered it with a cough. Then, putting on her best 'adult' voice she spoke:

'Oh excuse me! I'm a journalist from the... 'The Daily Chronicle' and I am ringing up about our recent competition...Talented Youth. You have a pupil at your school called....let me see...' Holly put in a dramatic pause to make it look like she was going through her paper-work but was instead slapping Jamie to stop him from laughing too loudly, as the game would then surely have been up! 'Oh here it is, Holly Fitzgerald, I believe she's in year 6?'

'Yes that's right. I'm sorry but the secretary is out at lunch at the moment and I'm a pupil who answers the phones for her. Is there an adult you would like to speak to?'

Holly, not expecting this, let her voice slip momentarily back to normal and replied. 'Oh no that's alright!' She quickly disguised her voice again and continued. 'I wonder if you would be kind enough to give her a message for me!'

'Yes I can do that!' replied Paul, oblivious to the sudden change in her voice.

'Can you tell her that she has been successful in reaching the singing finals with her song 'Defying Gravity' from the hit musical Wicked!'

'Really!' Paul couldn't disguise his excitement. 'Oh, sorry, yes I will give her the message.'

'Can you also add that she has the most fantastic voice that we have ever heard in the history of the competition and I'm sure...Ouch!!'

'Excuse me? Are you ok?'

Holly glared across at Kate who had just hit her for going over the top and was now urging her to end the call before she and the rest of them got found out.

'Yes, sorry I dropped a stapler on my toe! If you could pass that message on and please make sure no-one else finds out, as we need to keep it hush-hush if you know what I mean?'

'Yes certainly. Thank you for calling. Bye!' Holly closed her phone and slipped it back into her pocket before anyone saw she had her mobile out.

'Keeping it hush-hush! Where on earth did that come from?' laughed Max clutching his chest and laughing loudly. Next to him was Kate who was also laughing uncontrollably, doubled up with tears cascading down her cheek.

'I don't know. I saw it on a TV programme once!'

Everyone burst out laughing and congratulated Holly for completing her dare. They couldn't wait for Paul to give her the message after lunch. Holly then went into detail with the group describing exactly what Paul had said to her and his reaction on hearing the wonderful news.

The short dare recount ended with Holly telling Max he had come up with a great dare letting him know that if he ever wanted to be dare delegator, then he could do the job. Max, rather embarrassed by the compliment, smiled, said thank you and asked her more about the dare.

Unbeknown to either of them in deep discussion, Alfie was getting quite jealous of the attention Holly was giving to Max and not him. Alfie decided to break up their chat at once.

'Right, Holly's done her dare, now it's someone else's turn!'

Alfie captured Holly's interest again, along with everyone else in the group and they wondered who should be next.

# Chapter 4 - Lucky Dip Dare

Unsurprisingly no-one was interested in doing the next dare and everyone was looking everywhere except at each other.

'How about Hamster? He was interested in getting things moving along!' goaded Jamie, picking a stone out of his left shoe and flicking it at Alfie.

'Yeah, why not? Come on, let me know what I'm doing.' demanded Alfie. 'I'm right up for a challenge today. Lessons were so boring and I could have been practising my overhead kick by now!'

Alfie immediately demonstrated his spectacular overhead kick from his seated position. He rolled backwards, lifting his right leg above his head and, like a sling shot, his left leg swung up and over his head with amazing speed and grace. To Kate's untrained and uninterested eyes, it looked more like a beached whale had been stranded on a sandy beach, flapping its dorsal fin wildly in the air. Jamie and Max, both caught up in the moment, shouted GOAL and high-fived each other as though imagining the ball screaming past a stunned goal keeper into goal.

'Have you finished?' asked an unimpressed Holly, who had started to wonder why she ever allowed boys to join the group. It was going to be a girls only dare group until Kate pointed out that some dares would be better with boys in the group! 'I think we should have Lucky Dip Dares. We haven't done that in ages.'

Holly pulled out some small scraps of paper from her pocket and her combi-pen with a multitude of colours to choose from. 'Look, here's some paper and something to write with, Hamster, no peeking!'

Alfie scrunched up his eyes, which made his face look like a bulldog, and covered them with his hands to demonstrate to everyone that he wasn't looking. Everyone else in the group was busy thinking of an appropriate dare and when they had their light bulb moment, reached for a piece of paper and a pen, scribbling it down quickly.

‘Hand them back to me when you’ve finished.’ Holly told the group after completing her own dare and folding it neatly into a small square.

One by one the children finished secretly writing down their dares and folded their piece of paper in half and in half again, handing the folded pieces of paper back to Holly.

‘Ok Hamster you can open your eyes now.’

Alfie de-scrunched his face and glanced around the circle at all the smiling faces. Jamie had an unusually big grin on his face and gave Alfie a wink suggesting that his dare was going to be a great one!

Holly placed them all in her right hand and, after taking a peek at one of the pieces of paper not properly folded, put them behind her back smirking as she did this.

‘Now remember, it’s a process of elimination, so you’re going to have to do the last dare left in my hand.’

Holly wriggled on the spot so she was completely facing Alfie, who was sitting next to her, mixing the pieces of paper behind her like she was one of the National Lottery machines.

‘Come on, we don’t have long before lunch finishes.’ implored an excited and impatient Alfie.

Out of view of Alfie’s inquisitive eyes, Holly grasped two pieces of paper, one in each hand, and brought them out in front of her in clenched fists. ‘Which one?’ asked Holly with arms outstretched.

Alfie tapped Holly’s left hand. She turned it over and revealed the first piece of paper. Alfie picked it up, unwrapped it and read what it said to the rest of the group.

‘You have to tell Mr Jones that you love him!’ Everyone in the group laughed. ‘I’m glad I don’t have to do that one!’ Kate looked glum as it was her dare Alfie had read out and knew that it wasn’t going to be the dare he had to do.

Once again Holly rummaged behind her back and pulled out another two pieces of paper. Alfie chose the left hand again, thinking it was a lucky hand, and read out the dare after unfolding it.

‘You have to try on eight different pairs of glasses.’

Everyone stared at Max and then shook their head in disapproval of what they had just heard.

'Hey! How did you know it was my dare?' Max responded in disbelief.

'Because you're the only one who would have come up with such a lame dare!' retorted Kate.

'Well, I didn't have much time to think. It was the best I could do in the time.' Max crossed his arms, resigned to the fact that it was a lame dare, and thought of all the fantastic ones he should have written down.

'There are only three left Hamster. Make your next choice.'

Alfie carefully inspected each hand looking for any signs of paper sticking out and then decided to Ip Dip. 'Ip Dip Do, Mum's on the loo, Dad goes crazy out goes you.' Alfie tapped the right hand, picked up the crumpled piece of paper and read out the dare. 'You have to give someone in your class a wedgey.'

'Oh, I've been waiting ages to give someone that dare! I would have loved to have seen that!' Jamie called out, revealing that it was his dare. 'Oh well, I'd better get it out of my system.'

He quickly turned to Max who was sitting next to him, reached down and pulled up hard on his pants, giving him a moderate wedgey, as he was sitting down. Max screamed out in pain while shoving his hands unceremoniously down the back of his trousers, pulling and tugging at his pants to give him some relief in the pain department.

The group once again collapsed into fits of laughter while pointing at Max who was rolling around trying to return the string like pants to normal. Max soon found he was less restricted by his under garments, giving air back to vital parts of his body and decided to punch Jamie for the pain and humiliation.

'Idiot!' said Max.

Jamie rubbed his arm where he had just been punched but continued to smile knowing it had been very funny to watch and worth the resulting punch.

'Boys, come on now. We still have two dares left. Now choose the next one to get rid of. We're not supposed to know who wrote the dares but it looks like we've all forgotten that rule!' Holly gave everyone her sternest 'You Should Know Better' stare and held out her hands for Alfie to choose.

Alfie had worked out that he was left with Holly or Sophie's dare. He knew Holly's dare wasn't going to be easy as her dares were always challenging but didn't know what type of dare Sophie would write for him.

He looked at Holly as he waved his hand over the two choices left. He felt Holly knew which dare was in each of her hands, however she had her poker face on and wasn't letting on which hand hers was in.

Alfie was getting more worried; he didn't want Holly's dare and just as he was about to choose the right hand he thought he saw her mask crack and a little smirk start to form on her top lip. Alife changed his mind and touched her left hand. Holly let out a deflated sigh and opened her fist revealing her own dare.

'You chose my dare Hamster and you missed out on a great dare!'

Alfie, relieved that he had managed to side-step Holly's dare, read it out to the rest of the group. 'You are to lick the bottom of everyone's shoe! I hope you didn't mean the whole school!!' said Alfie inspecting the groups shoes a little more carefully. 'I'm so glad I don't have to do that, I'm not sure what that is on Jamie's shoe, but it doesn't look nice!'

Everyone stared at the bottom of Jamie's shoe where a red and green looking substance had embedded itself between the grooves of his shoe. Max wanted a closer look and pulled at Jamie's shoe, toppling him over as he gave it a sniff.

'Yep, that doesn't smell too nice either! So what's the dare Hamster has to do?' asked Max, now pinching the end of his nose whilst releasing the offending foot to the floor.

Alfie picked up the last remaining piece of paper, while noticing a small grin spread across Sophie's previously calm and stone-like face. He unfolded the piece of paper and simply stared at what was written across it.

'Come on, what does it say?' asked Jamie, snatching the piece of paper from Alfie's grasp and reading it aloud so the whole group could hear. 'You are to kiss 5 girls before the end of the day!' Jamie laughed and began taunting Alfie with little air kisses, fully expecting him to refuse to do it. However, to his surprise, Alfie quickly jumped to his feet and, with steely determination, ran away from Hugh and the circle of stunned faces.

'He's done a runner!' said Max, not quite understanding the sudden bizarre behaviour of his friend.

'No, he's doing the dare, he's going to kiss five girls.' assured Kate, who had turned quickly around not wanting to miss a second of the action. 'I wonder who he's going to kiss first.'

Alfie had darted off to Stumpy's old resting ground, where children were balancing on the beams, trying to get across without falling off; continuously summersaulting over and under the parallel bars until they became dizzy; suspended upside down viewing the world from a completely different perspective. Some, were acting like little monkeys swinging from one ring to the other with their other hand tucked under their armpit.

Alfie was looking all along the trim trial seeking out someone in particular. He didn't seem to find the person he was looking for, as he ran off towards the sensory and butterfly garden.

'I think he's lost it, he's trying to find a way out of the dare!' said Jamie, who, with the rest of the group, was now tracking Alfie's every move.

'No look, he's found a girl,' pointed out Sophie.

Although he was a long way off, it was clear to see that Alfie had grabbed a small girl in his arms and was giving her a bear hug, spinning her round and round. After appeared to be like four revolutions he put the girl down, kissed her on the cheek and ran back towards the flabbergasted group.

'I can't believe it! He's kissed the first of his girls. But why did he have to run all over the field to do it?' asked Max squinting trying to distinguish who the mystery girl was.

'I know who the girl is!' said Kate confidently.

Everyone spun their head, as if anyone could name a child over two hundred metres away under the glaring sun, it was going to be Kate.

It wasn't just faces she observed, as Kate spent many a lunch time talking to everyone in the school, usually to pass on her hot gossip, and had the innate ability to remember their style of hair whether short, long, spiked, curled, straightened or crimped. She could also remember if they were a fashion hit or a fashion miss by the accessories they wore. Did they still have the out-dated glitter gummy bracelets or the hip and trendy shell bead bangles that Kate could usually make at a fraction of the cost the high street stores were selling them at. The most distinguishing feature was what a person was wearing; did they have the latest checked summer dress or the pleated skirt and white blouse? She would even know if they were wearing the new style blue jumper with the logo on it or the long-sleeved unbranded jumper from Edwards and Co.

'It's Megan! Hamster's little sister.' revealed Kate.

‘That’s why he was running everywhere. He was looking for her. I will have to remember that next time I get dared to kiss anyone.’ said Max.

‘That would be fine but you have a brother not a sister!’ replied Kate.

Max was thinking through carefully what Kate had just told him, until it finally dawned on him what that would actually mean.

Alfie had now reappeared slightly out of breath and announced to the entire group. ‘That’s one girl down and four to go!’ He high fived Max and Jamie, who congratulated him on a very clever idea well executed and then looked at the three girls sitting opposite him. ‘Please forgive me for what I am about to do!’

Before Kate could ask what on earth he was on about, Alfie leapt over to her and planted a kiss on her cheek and in one swift movement swivelled around planting a kiss on Sophie’s nose (He had aimed for her cheek but Sophie had turned her head at the last moment resulting in a botched kiss).

Next on his kiss hit-list was Holly. If he hadn't paused to look at her, he would have found the next kiss a lot easier. However, making eye contact with Holly made things worse as he remembered how much he liked her and they were also on the verge of going out, even though it was all a misunderstanding! Thoughts raced through his head, the loudest of which being 'This could be your *first* kiss!'

In an instant it turned very awkward. Holly knew what was coming next and had wanted it more than life itself, but now it was becoming a reality doubt set in swiftly and she wondered if it was going to be as good as she had dreamed it would be.

With everyone looking and Sophie and Kate waiting expectantly for their plan to reach the next level, Alfie decided to just go for it, just like he had with the other girls. He bent down so his head was level with Holly's, licked his dry lips and planted a kiss on Holly's left cheek, lingering longer than he had with the other girls and then parted after what seemed to him like an eternity. He quickly turned away as if nothing had happened while Kate and Sophie closed in on Holly to discuss 'The Kiss'.

'There you go, four girls kissed. Now I've just got one more to kiss!'

Before Alfie had time to search out another girl a whistle blew three times, indicating it was the end of lunchtime and that everyone should stop what they were doing and line up; although a game of football always continued in to extra time as if a vital goal were needed.

'Balls!!' exclaimed Alfie as he knew the chances of completing the dare now were very poor.

The group picked themselves up off the grass, brushed themselves down and sauntered to the line of children waiting to go into class. The boys were consoling Alfie for not being able to complete the dare and the girls were still in deep discussion, analysing in detail what had just happened between Alfie and Holly.

# Chapter 5 - Maths Lesson

It wasn't long before the fun-filled lunchtime was replaced by the monotonous maths lesson. Jamie was sitting on the back row busily copying the difficult algebraic equations Miss Chalk was writing on the board at un-human speed, while Max, sitting next to him, was working at a snail's pace so that, by the time he had finished copying the questions from the board, Jamie would have hopefully already answered them all and give him the answers! Kate was sitting at the other end of the row looking very disheartened, having been moved from the back row for talking to Sophie too much, who was not liking her new partner, 'Perfect' Dave.

Kate's mind began to wander, as she wasn't in the mood for maths after feeling picked on for talking, and noticed that the front row always managed to get an easy sheet to work through instead of working from the board. She then thought back to the events over lunchtime when it had been so much fun sitting under Hugh with the rest of the gang coming up with dares.

Kate suddenly sat upright from her slouched position. If the dares could continue now, it would definitely brighten up her afternoon! She quickly rummaged through her particularly neat tray, tearing a scrap of paper from her homework book. She scribbled a message on the lined piece of paper with more enthusiasm than she had ever applied to her maths work, signing it off with her usual Kx and screwed it up into a small ball.

With a quick look to check that Miss Chalk was still on a mission to completely fill every inch of the board with mind blowing equations, she turned and tossed the small projectile which flew inches from Sally's head, skidding to a stop on Jamie's maths book. Kate mimed to Jamie that he should read the message before returning to look as though she were hard at work.

Jamie slid the crumpled piece of paper off his book, carefully unfolding and flattening it while an intrigued Max peered over his right shoulder. He read the message and decided to add his own before making a paper aeroplane out of it. Jamie needed it to reach Alfie and an aerodynamic plane would accomplish more than a screwed up piece of paper. Jamie took his creation between his thumb and forefinger, aimed at the large target of Alfie's head and released the jet fighter with a quick flick of his wrist.

The plane dipped and swayed across the classroom on its designated flight path until it nosedived and banked to the left, just short of its intended landing zone. Luckily, Sophie was on the ball, already preparing to grab the now spinning plane.

There was quite a bit of commotion along the back row as the plane swooped past Toby, narrowly missing Alice's hair bunches followed by quiet gasps fromMax and Jamie as the plane suddenly nose-dived out of control just before Sophie expertly caught it.

Miss Chalk was the first one to turn around and she scrutinised the back row for the cause of the disturbance. The entire back row was looking directly at Sophie, who, having followed the plane's flight path, was now hiding the paper aeroplane by sitting on it. She decided to cause a diversion by squeezing an ink cartridge, until it exploded in her pencil case.

With Miss Chalk now looking directly at her with a quizzical gaze, Sophie picked up her pencil case and showed a river of blue ink flowing over rubbers, pencils and pens. 'Miss, one of my ink cartridges has spilt in my pencil case. Can I go and wash it out please?

Miss Chalk thought that was a very good idea and told her she should go outside and clean it all up. Like a magician, Sophie picked up her pencil case, slipping the flattened paper aeroplane underneath, and walked out of class towards the toilets.

Upon her return, she decided to take the longer route back to her seat so that she could walk past Alfie and slip him the note which she had added to while outside. Without stopping or slowing down, Sophie bent over slightly and slipped the neatly folded piece of paper onto Alfie's maths book before continuing back to her seat.

As Alfie turned the piece of paper over, he noticed that Sophie had written on the front '4 ur Eyes Only! –

Sop'. He turned around and Sophie mouthed to him that he should open it. Alfie quickly opened the note and read it. It said:

Pass onto Hamster!

Kx – Time 2 complete ur dare?

Jam: 4 down 1 to go?

Yeah u gotta do it! – Sop

Taking his HB pencil and another piece of paper, Alfie wrote his reply 'I dont no how!!! – Hamster'. Alfie then folded the piece of paper into his hand and put his arm up in the air.

'Yes Alfie?' asked Miss Chalk.

'Can I get a ruler please?' said Alfie hoping that the answer would be yes.

'Yes but be quick about it.'

Alfie quickly got to his feet and walked around the table behind him, past Sophie and onto the last cabinet against the wall where the rulers were kept. It just happened to be where Max and Jamie sat too! As Alfie bent down to get a ruler, he dropped the piece of paper onto the floor.

Max spotted the drop and thought it was just like that secret agent film he watched last night where the spy dropped off secret intelligence at a newspaper stand before being shot by a hidden marksman. He hoped no sharpshooters would pick him off as he quickly scooped up the piece of paper and read it.

As Alfie lingered by the drawer, pretending to rummage through it looking for a ruler that wasn't dented or broken, Max whispered to him.

'You'll have to kiss someone in class!'

'What? Who?' whispered Alfie picking up a dented ruler.

'I don't know. I'll ask Kate.'

Max quickly wrote a note to Kate asking who Max should kiss for his dare, screwed it up into a ball and threw it at Kate who had been carefully following the action behind her.

Kate caught it with one hand, took a quick look towards Miss Chalk, as she didn't want to get two warnings in one lesson, and read the message. With Max, Jamie and Alfie all looking in her direction she signalled towards a small brown haired girl wearing glasses with freckles across her face, mouthing 'Ruth' to the boys.

They turned in unison towards Ruth as if controlled by a puppeteer. As if Alfie's expression wasn't enough on its own to tell Kate 'NO WAY!' he pushed two fingers into his mouth and mimed being sick, due to the allergic reaction he got when he thought of kissing Ruth.

Jamie and Max suddenly got back to work as they noticed there wasn't any more room on the board for Miss Chalk to write on and whispered to Alfie that he should return back to his place before being told off.

As Alfie passed Sophie she held out a piece of paper behind her for him to take. She had been following the goings on and had an idea herself as to who he should kiss. As Alfie took the piece of paper Dave spotted what was going on.

'You're not supposed to be passing messages in class. I'm going to tell Miss.' Dave had his hand half-way up when Sophie leaned in menacingly close to him.

'If you tell Miss, I won't tell you which equation you've got wrong!'

Dave never wanted to get anything wrong and quickly withdrew his hand, scanning his page for any mistake he might have made. When he found his error on question eight, he was rather disgruntled that Sophie was better at equations than him and he shifted his whole body so that he was facing away from her and covered up his book, which suited Sophie perfectly!

Alfie read what Sophie had written 'Ok, what about Sally, shes in ur row?'

Once sitting down, he wrote that he would think about it and gave it back to Sophie, who made sure the others knew her suggestion.

For everyone now involved in the improvised instant messaging, it seemed like hours waiting to see what Alfie would do next. It was actually after only ten minutes that Alfie rose from his seat and made his way to the back of the class again, deciding it was going to be easier to kiss Sally approaching from the other direction.

As he was squeezing along the back row of tables past Sophie, Jamie and Max, with his intended victim unaware she was about to be Alfie's prey, he brushed up against the Human Body science display set-up on the end of one of the wall cabinets. The Life sized torso of a Human *had* been sitting there complete and whole. After an Alfie sized nudge it was soon missing a liver, spleen and a large intestine, which happened to land on Toby's head, much to his disgust.

Luckily, none of the plastic parts had hit the model of the heart, sitting precariously next to it. Otherwise there would have been a tidal wave of small plastic parts, which usually happened on a regular basis, much to Miss Chalk's annoyance as she had to reconstruct the heart each time!

'Alfie Johnston, what are you doing out of your place again?' demanded Miss Chalk.

Alfie quickly thought up an excuse. 'I need to borrow a rub…

'That wasn't a question Alfie. Return to your place.' Miss chalk didn't look happy.

‘But…?’ Alfie tried his best to explain that he thought she had just asked him a question, when the ‘Mind Reading’ Miss Chalk retorted.

‘It was a rhetorical question, Alfie. Now return to your seat and get on with your work!’

He was confused by how Miss Chalk seemed to know that he was going to ask that exact question and wondered what other mysterious powers she had. Was she really of this world or the next? He knew he would have to speak to Greig, one of the Time Travellers, to see if he had similar thoughts or was he on his own?

Alfie continued to walk to the end of his row as his path was blocked by Alice and Toby who were trying to pick up the internal organs from the floor.

‘Look! Miss Chalk is looking for the instructions to put the body back together. You can still do it!’ Kate whispered to Alfie as he passed her on his way back to his chair. Alfie looked across to where Miss Chalk was now searching through her cupboard and knew this was the only opportunity he would get.

He turned along the next row. He took two steps to his right and pretended to trip over Kate's chair, clumsily stumbling forward, making a point to nudge Dave and in the process ruining his work, and then fell dramatically onto Sally. Alfie puckered up his lips and kept his eye on Sally's check like a guide missile. He managed to get a grip on the back of her chair, slowing his desent and planted a kiss firmly on her cheek. It was an Oscar winning performance but one Sally would not be voting for.

Sally man-handled Alfie from his position sprawled across her. 'Miss! Alfie has just kissed me!' she cried.

The whole class stopped what they were doing, quickly turned their heads, looked at the commotion behind them. As if at a tennis match, watching the ball being returned over the net, the class turned their heads again to see Miss Chalk's reaction.

'Alfie! Did you just kiss Sally?' Miss Chalk boomed. The ball had been returned with venom and the class swivelled their heads looking for the response.

'Miss, there is no-way on earth I would want to kiss Sally! No offence.' He said turning to a disgruntled

Sally. 'I lost my balance and had no control of any part of my body as I fell. We might have bumped heads but that's it!'

'Please apologise to Sally and quickly return to your place. You have a lot of work to catch-up on and if you don't get it done you will have extra homework! And that goes for the rest of you too!' threatened Miss Chalk, regaining control of the class and returning everyone's attention back to the maths work they still had to do.

Alfie apologised to Sally, who quickly dismissed it and returned to her work. He then managed to give two secret high fives to Max and Jamie before returning to his chair to finish his maths.

The rest of the maths lesson passed without incident and Alfie managed to complete the required amount of sums. The same could not be said for Kate, who only managed to complete three equations and would have to stay in during tomorrow's playtime to complete them.

Jamie-Lee asked to ring the bell to signal the end of the day and everyone packed up their books, fetched their bags and waited patiently behind their chairs to be dismissed.

Kate and Sophie were the last two to return from the cloakroom as Kate was moaning outside about the unfairness of having to stay in at playtime when Charles, who sat in front of her, had only completed two and didn't have to stay in!

'Good afternoon class 6!' said Miss Chalk after waiting for the last few to return.

'Good afternoon Miss Chalk, good afternoon everyone!' replied the class, bundling their way to the door and sending a few chairs toppling off the desk.

'Be careful with your bag Max!' shouted Miss Chalk as Max quickly disappeared out of the door without a backward glance.

## Chapter 6 - The Bird In The Woods

The sun was still shining high in the sky as Kate, Holly and Sophie walked across the busy playground. Little children raced around with their toilet roll rockets made earlier that day. Parents were busy catching up on playground gossip; some boys began a game of football with a half-eaten sponge ball and tied up dogs barked for their owners whilst tethered outside the school gate. The girls were old enough to walk home on their own and they made their way towards the gate at the far end of the railings.

'Hey look, there's Hamster!' pointed Kate eagerly, 'Why don't we go and speak to him, Holly?'

Alfie was in deep discussion with Greig in playground, explaining his theory that Miss Chalk was not from this planet and asking if Greig or any of the other 'Time Travellers' had noticed this.

‘I’ve changed my mind about Alfie.’ replied Holly, walking away from him.

‘Why? What’s happened? You really liked him earlier.’ queried Sophie.

‘That was before the slobbery kiss he gave me at lunchtime. It was worse than being kissed by my Grandpa when he’s not got his teeth in!’

‘Urgh!’ uttered both girls, screwing up their faces in disgust, imagining a toothless kiss.

‘My little brother used to give me slobbery kisses. His dribble used to run down my face. It was disgusting!’ said Kate, wiping her face even though nothing was there. ‘So I totally understand what you’re talking about. Do you want to walk through the woods with me and Sophie?’

There were two choices if you wanted to reach the Croft Wood estate, where Kate and the others lived. You could either take the very long winding path up towards the main road and follow it along the small high street, past the butchers, village store (including the post office and pick-a-mix sweet counter!). Then turn left just past the Fox and Hound pub, into the estate. It would usually take a good ten to fifteen minutes, or longer if you were stopping off to buy sweets.

The other, quicker alternative and a popular choice for most children was to turn left and take the woodland path through what was left of Croft Wood, after they had built the housing estate.

You could walk through Croft Wood in about five minutes, but most people would take a leisurely stroll through the woods or stop to play on the mini woodland adventure fort. The village council had built it last year, using the wood from the trees toppled after the hurricane; the same storm that brought down Stumpy.

They had gone into St Marks' to ask the children what they would like in the woods to make it more fun and update the falling apart play equipment already in place. There were lots of suggestions from a tree top walk-way to a giant pirate ship. However, the council decided on a climbing fortress with three large towers connected on one side by a three metre long swing bridge and, on the other side, a tunnel. There were many different ways to get up or down including a climbing wall, spiral slides, gang planks and a fireman's pole. They had also installed some traditional swings and a large nest swing, for the older children, which Jamie and nine of his friends managed to bundle on, one day last week, beating the previous record of eight.

As well as the large play area off to the right, to the left of the main path was a smaller, narrower path that branched off towards the woodland pond, before returning to the main path further up. It was a large pond and many school classes were bought here regularly to do some pond dipping or habitat studies, as it offered a wide variety of insects and pond life to study.

Holly agreed to walk with the girls through the woods, especially as she saw Alfie further up the main path, heading towards the shops, and she didn't want to see him again so soon. Not after that kiss!

'Why don't we go and have a look at the pond?' suggested Sophie, already turning left onto the narrow path without waiting for a response.

Both girls agreed and dashed to catch Sophie along the soft wood chipped path.

It wasn't long before they reached the pond and the locked gate, which was more for show than to actually prevent people getting into the pond area, as it was easy enough for anyone to duck between the horse pen style boundary fences. They were made with a medium sized log cut in half, which made the smooth topped hand rail, a metre from the ground. With another wooden bar attached half way between the floor and the top bar, allowing enough space for a giant to crawl through it.

After ducking through the fence, it was a short walk to a large expanse of sparkling water. The pond was about twenty five metres across at its widest part, and was oval shaped. Around its edges were sweet scented rush plants with sword like leaves which were covered in little red flowers, long grassy green leaves with brown sausage like seeds and also plants that masked the edge of the pond, speckled with tiny bright blue flowers. At intervals, little wooden platforms had been constructed enabling you to go right up to the water's edge without slipping and sliding on the muddy banks.

The girls could see pond skaters skimming quickly across the smooth still water between a variety of coloured water lily leaves and a rainbow of different coloured flowers floating on the water's surface. Dragon flies darted and weaved in and out of the long thin reeds and great crested newts swam between the plants occasionally popping their head above the surface. It was as tranquil and serene as a picture postcard. That was until each of the three girls had picked up a small stone and tried to skim it across the top of the water, disturbing the insects both above and below.

They skirted further around the pond, picking up more small stones and throwing them as far as they could, creating circular patterns in the murky blue water.

Sophie ran ahead of the others, as she noticed something interesting on the other side of the pond.

'Hey, look at all these feathers!' screamed Sophie, signalling to the other two to join her.

Kate and Holly ran to where Sophie was picking through a pile of soft pigeon feathers and then thought twice about joining in. Holly let out a small scream upon realising some of the feathers were covered in blood then she a ripped off claw with the leg bone protruding from the wrinkled skin. She immediately turned away in disgust.

Sophie was fascinated with the foot, pulling apart its toes and feeling how sharp its claws were, ignoring the muffled screaming sounds coming from Holly. Kate, although not overly keen on blood, guts and gore, had been friends with Sophie long enough, to know what she was like and had seen far worse in the past. Only last week they had come across a dead squirrel that Sophie had put in her empty lunch box and taken home!

Sophie lifted up the mutilated parts of the bird, brushing off the odd maggot so Kate could get a better look. 'Look, you can see where the wing has been bitten off!'

Sophie always had an unusual fetish for all things wriggly, small or dead and was often the first to pick up a worm or slug, which she would do frequently when playing over at Kate's to annoy her irritating brothers. She even once tried to resuscitate a dead mouse by giving it chest compressions but was luckily prevented from giving it mouth-to-mouth when her mum called her in for dinner!

'How can you bear to touch that?' asked Holly, looking over Kate's shoulder, hoping not to see any further bloodshed but catching sight of the single blooded wing.

'Oh come on, it's only a bit of blood,' reasoned Sophie, picking up the other half of the wing and waving it in front of Holly, who quickly retreated behind Kate. 'The body must be around here somewhere. I don't think the fox would have taken it far!'

Sophie crawled along the floor, following the feather trail a metre or so further through the brambles and weeds. 'I've found it! Do you want to come and see it? You can see right into its chest!'

Holly tried everything she could not to be sick and said she would stay by the pond, away from the carnage. Kate, more intrigued than Holly, hopped over the brambles into the small clearing where she could see the carcass of a bird laying on the leaf and moss covered ground. By now, Sophie had picked up two small sticks and was prodding the bird from all sides, pulling and scraping out its small intestine and what looked like its damaged rib cage.

'If I can find its head, I'm going to take it home!' announced Sophie, putting the stick down and looking around for the bird's decapitated head.

'Hey, I've got an idea. Find that head and I'll be back in a minute!' Kate returned to where Holly was sitting, throwing stones into the pond and trying to wipe all the memories of what she had just witnessed from her mind.

'Holly, are you up for a dare?'

Holly turned and looked up at Kate. 'What is it? I don't have to eat anything do I?'

'You have to agree to the dare first! And no you won't have to eat anything. I promise.' Kate crossed her heart with her fingers and waited for Holly's reply.

Unsure what she might be letting herself in for she agreed to do the dare, but was a little frightened at what Kate might have planned for her. Kate took Sophie's hand

and guided her back to the clearing where Sophie was now holding something behind her back.

'So what's....urgh look at that!' Holly had just spotted the recently dissected bird's chest and covered her mouth and nose, with her free hand trying again to prevent her being sick.

'Yeah, it's cool, isn't it! Look at this.' Sophie said revealing the bird's head which she had been holding behind her back.

Holly looked at the small grey feathered head and thought how cute the bird was. Then she realised it was just the head and nearly fainted.

Once she had regained her composure, her thoughts turned to what the dare might be. 'What am I being dared to do, Kate?'

'I dare you to hold the bird's head and open up its beak!'

'You mean I have to touch that horrible, diseased thing!' Holly pointed towards the head, still lying on Sophie's hand.

Kate and Sophie both nodded their heads.

‘Have we not had enough of dares for one day?’ pleaded Holly.

‘No! Come on are you chicken or something? I dare you to pick up the bird’s head and open its beak.’

At that moment Holly understood what peer pressure felt like and didn’t want her friends to think she was a chicken. She reluctantly reached out and took hold of the bird’s head between her trembling fingers.

It was soft to the touch and very light. She could feel the skull bone through its light grey feathers and thought about running away and throwing up. However, Holly maintained her composure and, keeping the head in one hand, she used her finger and thumb to hold the bottom of the beak and, with her other hand, took hold of the top beak. It was really fiddly as it was so small but when she thought she had a good enough grasp she glanced towards Kate and Sophie, who had moved in for a closer look, and they nodded that she could now open it up!

Holly closed her eyes and slowly pulled the two parts of the beak apart. They moved surprisingly easily, as she felt the hinge of the jaw moving up and down.

After Sophie had mentioned how cool it was, Holly decided to have a peek at the bird and thought she saw a minute red tongue move around in its mouth. Holly shivered and immediately dropped the head to the floor, wiped her hands quickly on her summer dress and stepped away to control her fast breathing.

Kate congratulated Holly for being really brave and completing the dare. 'Well done Holly! You're a braver girl than me. I don't think I would have done it!'

'That's the worst thing I've ever done.' Holly began to walk back to the pond, leaving Sophie and Kate to prod and poke the head some more. Upon reaching a comfortable distance, she stopped and turned back to face the CSI of the bird world. 'I think it's only fair that, as I've done a dare, you two should do one too.'

'What do you have in mind, Holly?'

Holly thought for a moment, glanced behind her towards the pond to confirm her initial idea and then turned back around, smiling. 'I think you should both wade to the middle of the pond!

Sophie and Kate both looked at each other and nodded in silent agreement.

'Ok, we'll do it!' said Kate shaking hands with Holly to seal the deal.

'That was easy!' said Holly thinking it was *too* easy to get them to do it.

'Well it's only fair isn't it? We dared you and you did it, even though you hated it. So there's no-way we could back out of a dare.' replied Sophie, getting to her feet and abandoning the bird.

The trio made their way to the bank of the pond. Kate and Sophie sat down and started to take off their school shoes and white socks, placing them in neat piles on the wood chipped path. Kate was first to finish and dipped her toe into the pond, testing the temperature. It was surprisingly chilly! Sophie was soon ready and joined Kate by the water's edge.

‘After three we’ll both step in together,’ Kate suggested looking down through the clear water to the mud filled bed below. ‘One…two…three!’

Both girls slowly put one foot into the pond, feeling its icy cold water chill their toes. As the water reached their ankles they felt the thick slimy mud of the pond bed creep up around their feet and squeeze through their toes. With one foot firmly stuck in the mud their free foot soon joined it in the now murky water.

Sophie started off towards the centre of the pond, holding Kate’s hand, as she struggled to pull her feet from the mud prison surrounding them. As she got further away from the edge of the pond it was easier to move, and Kate was slowly following behind her.

After about four or five steps they soon noticed they were on a slight slope, as the water was gradually getting deeper and was soon up around the bottom of their knees. Both girls by now had a tight hold of their rolled up skirt and summer dress, making sure it didn’t drop into the rising water.

From the side, Holly was following their progress. They were about half way to the middle when she noticed that the water was darker in the middle than at the side but couldn't work out why.

'Hey Kate, I hope it doesn't get any deeper. I'm not as tall as you!' said Sophie, noticing that the water had already covered her knees and seemed to be getting deeper.

'Don't worry, I've got a good hold of you. I won't let you fall in, I promise!'

Sophie, encouraged by her friend's words of reassurance, slowly used her left foot to probe the water in front of her, testing how deep it was going to get. She felt the cold water pass completely over her knee and rise up her thigh. Her foot continued to drop further and she still hadn't reached a hard surface. The bottom of her skirt was now absorbing the pond water, turning the bottom an even darker shade of grey as she had let go of it in order to keep her balance.

Sophie lowered her foot an extra few centimetres, hoping to find the bottom of the pond but instead ended up treading water and she began to lose her balance. Kate tightened her grasp on Sophie's white blouse as she had promised, keeping her upright and stopping her from taking an early bath.

'It's too deep! I think it will go above my waist!' Sophie shouted out to Holly, safe on the dry bank of the pond.

'Ok, you don't have to go any further. You've completed the dare. Come back now!' urged Holly worried that Sophie was about to fall in.

The girls swung around and made their way back safely to the water's edge. Just as they put one foot on the dry bank they heard someone shouting at them to get out of the pond.

Holly helped Kate out of the pond first, followed by a dripping Sophie. They both quickly put on their shoes, shoving their socks into their pockets, beginning to worry who had seen them wading into the pond.

With their bags slung over their shoulders they ran towards the entrance of the pond to make a quick escape.

‘Come on Holly, I can hear them coming around the corner!’ urged Kate, throwing her bag over the fence while helping Holly duck under the barrier. Sophie had decided to vault over the gate further down the path and was picking up her bag when she saw Max and Jamie walk around the bend laughing their heads off!

‘Ha! Ha! It was only us. Don’t worry. What on earth are you lot doing?’

The two boys looked strangely at the sockless girls. Sophie’s skirt was dripping wet and her legs were covered in slime and pondweed. Kate was checking out the pond life that had set up home on her legs and pulling off the thick sticky mud.

‘We were doing dares.’ replied Sophie as she re-joined the group. ‘We had to stand in the middle of the pond after we dared Holly to open up a dead bird’s mouth!’

‘Oh! Why didn’t you wait for us? We could have joined you and made it more fun!’ joked Max.

Kate had just picked off a sizable lump of mud from her leg and she threw it at the laughing Max, who spotted the missile and quickly ducked out of the way. That's when they realised that Rachel Webb, one of their classmates, was walking up behind them to see what was going on.

The mud that had just missed Max, hit Rachel squarely on the side of her face, splattering on her cheek. As the force of gravity took effect, it slid down her face, fell to the floor and left a brown streak and fowl pond smell.

Kate quickly ran up to Rachel, pulled out a tissue and, while profusely apologising, wiped her face. The boys were once again in stitches, laughing until Kate placed the blame squarely on Max's shoulders.

'Hey it wasn't my fault!' protested Max.

Kate took hold of Rachel's arm, ignoring the protest and walked with her along the path. Jamie could have sworn he heard her saying that boys are more trouble than they are worth, before she was out of audible range. Sophie and Holly quickly joined Kate after waving goodbye to the boys.

'The cheek of it! It wasn't even my fault and I'm the one who feels guilty. How does Kate do that?'

Both boys picked up their bags and wandered off along the path, discussing the prospects of seeing a fantastic match between Manchester United and Arsenal on television later that night and wondering who would score first.

# Chapter 7- The Unbreakable Triple Dare

**Thursday: The Unbreakable Triple Dare Day**

'Can you believe it? 5-1 to Man U? What were Arsenal doing? If only..'

Jamie cut short his rant to Max about the awful game he's see last night when he saw Kate coming out of the classroom, after finishing her detention with Miss Chalk.

They both ran up to the freed detainee to find out what had happened to Rachel, as she wasn't in school that day and guiltily thought it had something to do with getting mud on her face. Max thought she had caught swamp fever from all the toxins in the pond. Jamie wanted to find out the truth and asked Kate directly.

'Hey Kate, do you know what's happened to Rachel?'

'Yeah, has she got deadly swamp fever and been rushed to hospital?' asked Max, hoping he was right in his diagnosis.

'No, she hasn't got swamp fever!' Kate shook her head in disbelief. 'She's gone for a drama scholarship at Ferndale Grammar School for Girls this morning. She was fine about everything yesterday and did see the funny side of it. But she still wasn't happy with you Max!'

Max was on the verge of giving Kate a piece of his mind about the unfairness of it all, when he saw her smile and then laugh. 'Don't worry, I'm just kidding you. I told her the truth and apologised to her.'

As Kate looked at her watch, to see how much play she had left, the lunchtime supervisor blew the whistle. Everyone lined up in military fashion waiting for their teacher to come out and tell them that they could go in!

The next lesson they had was Art, which cheered Kate up as she loved the subject. Today's lesson involved a still life portrait drawing so all the tables had been arranged into a circle with a chair placed in the centre.

Each place had a large piece of paper and a drawing pencil lying next to it. Miss Chalk instructed everyone to find a seat around the edge and introduced the lesson. Rachel was chosen to go and sit on the chair in the middle as the class model and looked very excited about this.

Rachel thought of herself as a pretty girl, and most of the boys wouldn't have disagreed. She thought that one day she could become a famous model and decided that this was her opportunity to take her first steps towards the Milan Fashion Show. She walked to the chair and took up a very extravagant pose before being told that she had to hold it for an hour, at which point she opted for a more comfortable position.

For the next hour the class sat silently drawing Rachel from their point of view, so that no picture was identical. There was a big moan half-way through the lesson when Rachel couldn't resist scratching her nose which she meant she had to move and then never quite returned to the exact position she had held before.

The second interruption came from Miss Chalk as she asked Max why there was a big smudge on his drawing of Rachel's face. He replied that he could see a smudge of dirt on her cheek and thought he should include it in his drawing. Miss Chalk couldn't see any dark mark on Rachel's face and asked him to rub it out and to be more observant in future.

Everyone who had been at the pond yesterday afternoon, including Rachel, knew he had drawn the mud splattered face and began giggling, confusing Miss chalk as to why her comment was so funny. Also, Rachel managed to once again annoy everyone in class as she was doubled up in fits of laughter.

The rest of lesson proceeded as Miss Chalk had planned and everyone was proud of their drawings, although Rachel couldn't understand what some of them had been looking at, as some of their pictures didn't make her look beautiful and some looked nothing like her!

After a huge clear up, returning the tables and chairs back to how they were, the lunch time bell could be heard ringing in unison with many rumbling stomachs. The usual lunchtime routines were observed, and everyone took up their usual places in the dinner hall apart from Alfie, who was missing from the footy team table as he had been invited to sit with the 'Time Travellers' to discuss his 'Miss Chalk is an Alien' theory.

Once they were dismissed from the lunch hall, a wave of children hit the field, scattering in all directions like a tsunami. Children of all sizes picked up skipping ropes, added the finishing touches to grass houses or set up goal posts with their jumpers. Six children broke away from the rest of the juniors and made a bee line towards Hugh, with Jamie at the front and Kate and Sophie bringing up the rear.

The lunchtime supervisors were on their customary circuit of the field, patrolling all areas, including Hugh, so dare making was put on hold until the coast was clear. The girls pulled out a magazine and began reading about the recent Blue Star concert while Sophie kept saying how gorgeous they all were. A game of Rock, Paper, Scissors was being played by the boys with Alfie taking an early lead.

After the lunchtime supervisor had observed the children playing nicely under the shade of the large tree, she moved hastily off towards the sensory garden where a couple of year three boys had caught hold of a worm!

'I think its Kate's turn for a dare if I remember rightly.' said Holly after the lunchtime supervisor was out of earshot.

'Didn't I do one yesterday after school?' queried Kate, hoping to get out of doing the dare.

'That doesn't count. We weren't all there,' replied Holly.

'Yeah, no mention to me that you were going to the pond!' said Alfie, feeling left out having gone home via the sweet shop.

Holly looked down at the floor knowing the real reason for not speaking to Alfie as Jamie spoke out. 'We called out to you but it looked like you were on a mission to get to the sweet shop first.'

'I was! They were getting in the new black drum of Toxic Waste Sour Sweets,' said a very excited Alfie. 'They were mind blowing. I could only keep one in my mouth for 20 seconds before my eyes watered and the back of my tongue felt like it was going to explode. You've gotta try it!'

They all began to ask more details about the new Toxic Waste sweets. 'Well, we can talk about that later, right now we have more important things to discuss than that,' interrupted Holly.

'Like what?' asked Jamie.

'Dares!'

'Oh yeah, sorry!'

Now that order had been restored, Holly looked at Kate. 'I dare you to run around the field telling everyone that you are an alien and make up a silly dance to go with it.'

Everyone nodded in agreement thinking it was a good dare and then waited for Kate's reaction.

'I accept!'

Kate jumped up to her feet and, in front of the group, said 'I'm an alien! I'm an alien! I'm an alien!' while waving her arms wildly about, wiggling her hips and then jumping up and down on the spot. The whole group found it very amusing. Kate then wandered off to repeat the whole routine to as many people as she could.

She got some very strange reactions, especially from the boys trying to play football who found she was just getting in the way of a good game. The best reaction came from the lunchtime supervisors. Kate, now getting used to embarrassing herself, had told them she was an alien and they replied 'That's very nice Kate, thank you for telling us', and carried on as normal!

After Kate had made her way around the entire field, she returned, quite exhausted, and collapsed onto the floor next to Sophie whilst everyone congratulated her for an outstanding alien impression.

'So, who will be next, as I have another great dare?' Holly announced to the group.

'It's Jamie's turn next. All he had to do last week was call Miss Chalk 'Mum' during lesson time! Even I did that by mistake yesterday!'

'Okay. What is it?' asked Jamie, feeling quite guilty, as he knew he had been given an easy dare last time.

‘The double dare came to me when I was in the cloakroom yesterday. You have to go into the class cupboard and change into my spare summer dress and bra. Then, at the end of lunch time, go into registration still wearing it!

‘What! I’m no girl!’ Jamie spurted out.

‘Are you saying you’re not going to take the Double Dare!’

‘Yes! There’s no-way I’m wearing a bra! I’m the captain of the school football team. You can just imagine all the grief I’ll get on the field ‘Oh, you kick like a girl, oh, sorry you are one!’ or ‘Shouldn’t you be the captain of the Netball team?’ No way! Never! Absolutely NOT!’

Jamie thumped the floor so hard he left a fist impression in the dry mud. He immediately looked towards Max for support but found none. Max was looking at him a loss for words, deciding whether to side with Jamie, whilst also imagining his best friend in a dress. It was a tough choice!

Jamie, realising he wasn't going to get any support, crossed his arms across his chest and looked determinedly at Holly.

'Remember, if you refuse to do this, you'll have to take the Unbreakable Triple Dare!'

As Holly spoke those hallowed three words everything turned eerily silent. Jamie's heart beat quickened as he looked around from one shocked face to another. No-one spoke; it was as if someone had just sworn in class. Holly looked calmly around and smiled at Jamie. The eager crowd looked on, listening attentively to the choice he would make.

'Nope, I'm not doing it. Give me whatever consequence you want but I'm not dressing up as a girl, especially not with one of your bras!'

Holly looked around her, checking if she had the support of her group to continue, knowing they would have to back her up with the triple dare, then she continued. 'Okay. As you have decided to pass on the Double Dare, you will have to...' She paused for greater effect as everyone listened intently to Jamie's sentence, like a defendant waiting to hear the jury's verdict. '... to do 'The Unbreakable Triple Dare! As you know, this has only been attempted once before and we all...'

'Yeah, yeah, we all know that! Tell us what the dare is!' interrupted Kate impatiently. She knew this would make the best gossip ever!

'Okay, I *was* getting there! You have to hide in the class cupboard at the end of the day and stay at school *all* night!'

It was like a strange dream to Jamie as the words tumbled round and round in his brain not really comprehending them at first. But as it slowly dawned on him what she had just said, he tried to respond.

'You want me....The Triple Dare is to....at school all night...but...all night?'

'Yes you have to stay at school all night by yourself. You were the one that wanted to take the triple instead of the double!'

Now fully aware of the gravity of the situation, and slowly regaining his composure, Jamie asked anxiously. 'I don't have any choice do I?'

'Nope, you signed the dare contract and swore on the bible!'

This was something each member of the group had to do before they joined the dare game. Holly had borrowed the class bible the first lunchtime they had decided to play dares and had made everyone, with one hand on their heart and the other on the bible, promise that they would follow the rules of the game. They had then been forced to reveal one piece of very personal or embarrassing information with the rest of them. If they broke the rules everyone in school would find out their hidden secrets and they would be thrown out of the group.

'Ok, I wish I didn't have to do it, but I will.'

At this point Sophie let out a huge belly laugh. 'Haha! You should have taken up the first dare! I would have dressed up as a boy without any hesitation!' Sophie continued to laugh and roll around on the ground pointing at Jamie. That is until she heard what Holly had to say next.

‘I triple dare you to do it too, if you think it’s so funny that Jamie has to do it!’

It was unusual for Holly to be so vocal in Jamie’s defence but the memory of being taunted with the dismembered bird’s wing yesterday was still out the forefront of her mind and she saw her chance for revenge and seized it.

Sophie stopped laughing immediately, sat up slowly and looked at Jamie, pale and shocked, knowing there was no way out for her too.

# Chapter 8 - The Cupboard

**Thursday – 7pm.**

In the pitch blackness of the classroom, the only light available to the two dare attendees, was trapped inside the classroom cupboard. That's if you could call it a light, as the bulb was so dim and covered in years' worth of dust it barely lit the contents of the cupboard, and couldn't reach beyond its cramped confines.

Sophie was still rubbing her head while rummaging through the pile of books which now lay scattered on the floor, trying to find the offending book which had hit her head. She wanted to prove to Jamie that she wasn't just making a fuss about the bump on her head and that it was a rather large book that had hit her.

Ignoring the moans and groans coming from the cupboard, Jamie stood a couple of steps from Sophie, imagining the layout of the classroom and trying to plot a route through the semi-darkness to the classroom door, leading out to the corridor.

As Jamie's eyes began to focus and seek out glimmers of light, he could just make out an outline of the sink which he knew still had all the dirty brushes and paint pots that they had used in the art lesson earlier that day.

In the distance, on the wall, he noticed a small red glow surrounded by a ring of green light. Jamie froze as there had always been talk from the 'Time Travellers' that behind the 'Eye of the Board' lived a mechanical robot droid which spied on the classroom and protected it during the night. The headmaster also denied the rumour that video cameras were installed in each board or that the school was trialling the latest military security devices. However, that didn't stop Greig telling everybody that an evil eye was always looking out into the classroom and that, during the night, it searched for any signs of life to obliterate with its high powered green laser gun – which, if you were normal, you knew was the logo of Sight and Sound Interactive!

Jamie found the light useful as it gave him a reference point. He knew that the door to the corridor was at the end of the wall opposite the whiteboard. After getting his bearings, he started for the door. 'Sophie, stay close and follow me across the room.'

It wasn't an easy journey, bumping into various desk corners resulting in many bruises. With his hands outstretched, in attempt to avoid any more tables, he found the classroom globe and located what he thought was America, though it was difficult to be sure in the dark. It sat on display on top of the cupboard above their Maths and English book trays, which sat against the opposite wall. He used the edge of the cupboard like a guide dog leading the blind and made his way to the exit, narrowly missing the 3D model heart which was perched at the end of the next cupboard, and always seemed to fall apart at the slightest touch.

Just before he reached the door Jamie turned around, realising that there wasn't another pair of footsteps following his. A pair of footsteps belonging to Sophie. She wasn't following him! Jamie was annoyed as he had made good progress towards the door and he thought she was probably still fussing over the bump on her head.

'Sophie, what are you doing? If you're not going to go home and explain to your parents why you aren't staying at Kate's house, let's go and explore the rest of the school. Come on! Follow my voice.'

Sophie took a moment to think of a good retort from across the classroom, as she never wanted to lose an argument. However, she *had* lied to her parents and the thought of the trouble she could be in if she returned home, having *not* been at Kate's house, kept her lips securely shut and she started her walk into the darkness.

'Oh, and watch out for the 3D model...'

Jamie was caught mid-sentence by a clattering of tiny plastic parts hitting the worktop and rolling off onto the carpet with a dull thud.

'Sorry, what did you say? I've just knocked into that ghastly model of a heart! Can't you turn the lights on so we're not stumbling around like fools in the darkness?'

'Mr Jones has turned off the master switch. My Dad worked on the wiring of the new ceilings and told me he put in a master switch so Mr Jones could turn off all the lights from one place.'

Sophie, still groping in the darkness and moving slowly towards Jamie, continued her interrogation.

'But how come the cupboard light works?'

'It's only works where they've got the new false ceilings. They're doing the other rooms and cupboards during the Christmas break. Now come on!'

Both dare attendees pulled open the thick wooden door and looked out along the corridor checking for any signs of life, but all that could be heard was the ticking of a clock, back in the classroom, at its usual dull and boring pace. If you dropped a pin then you'd be able to hear its echo reverberating along the corridors long after it landed. Usually, it was day time and there was plenty of light; now all they could see was a strange landscape of dark semi-hidden and eerily shaped objects protruding from the wall, lit only from the skylights above inviting the moon light in.

Jamie tentatively began his walk along the moonlit corridor into the darker depths of the school. His heart was beating faster with each step. A toxic mix of excitement, nerves and apprehension filled every throbbing vein in his body, willing him to move on yet resisting each and every muscle pull. What if Mr Jones was somewhere in the building? What if they were not the only intruders to the school that evening? What would happen if they got caught?

While battling his body's urge to turn him into a nervous wreck, Jamie tried to concentrate on acting fearless as he didn't want Sophie to think he was a wimp. No first team footballer could be called a wimp! He had many scars on his legs, from career ending tackles, to prove that point.

With the dim moonlight diminishing as they progressed along the corridor, their path only lit by a red glow, emanating from a single false ceiling light, highlighting the emergency fire route out of the school.

Sophie had never seen this light before and was transfixed as though being probed by a spy robot delving into her deepest darkest thoughts and memories. A shiver shot down her spine jolting her back to reality and moving her away from her hidden secrets.

Emerging from the red glow, Jamie looked to his left and flinched slightly as he stared at scarily deformed and grotesque faces, each one framed individually. He bravely re-opened his eyes, allowing them to focus more clearly on the photographs before him and it dawned on him that he must be looking at the staff pictures on display by the school office. Sophie confirmed his conclusion after running her hands over the embossed sign, like she was reading brail.

'We're next to the School office, I can feel it!'

'If we're by the school office then we haven't got very far. Come on, keep moving!'

'Far to what? Where *are* we heading towards Jamie?'

'You'll know when we get there. Now, come on!'

It all looked very different, with darkness surrounding them, concealing familiar walls, objects and a welcoming environment. With limited light, the usual school posters could be seen with their positive messages:

‘The hands of friendship have no colour’, ‘Respect: Give it. To get it.’ And ‘Success comes in cans not cannots!’ Some posters had images of famous people staring menacingly out following the their every step.

‘I'm sure those posters are staring at me. They scare me!’ winced Sophie, moving herslef ever closer to Jamie.

‘Don't be silly, they were there this afternoon and didn’t follow you.’ assured Jamie.

‘Look, I just saw that runner’s eyes twitch!’

‘It’s just your imagination running wild. Look, there’s the corner up ahead, I’m sure they can’t see around corners unless they are like the pictures at Hogwarts!’ Jamie let out a little laugh, picturing Jonathan Edwards triple jumping from one picture to the next or Chris Hoy cycling through the school photo, past all the sitting teachers and into the middle of a Lacrosse match.

They turned the corner and found themselves in complete darkness. A few steps further down the corridor and they could just about see their hand in front of them. Sophie's heart-beat was matched by the dripping of a nearby tap. Edging slowly forward, Jamie felt his shirt being pulled from behind and knew Sophie felt as he did, frightened!

Jamie felt his way past the lost property box which had spilled out over the edge and cluttered the floor. He could make out a long soft scarf, a woolly hat with a frizzy bobble on top, a lone smelly plimsoll and even a plastic water bottle. Feeling his way up along the smooth brick wall, he fumbled around for the cloakroom hooks which would lead them along like stepping stones across a river. His warm hand found the cold metal bar protruding at a strange angle from the wall and he groped in the darkness to find the next one. His hand found an abandoned coat but knew a hook was beneath the thick fur lined hood and continued carefully onto the next one.

Following closely behind, Sophie wasn't as careful and, unaware of the lost property littering the ground in front of her, stepped onto the empty water bottle which let out an alarming high pitched squeak.

'Ahhhh! Mouse! RUN!' screamed Sophie.

'What...' Jamie didn't have time to reply as before he knew it, he was being pushed blindly through the darkness by two small hands from behind him. He was out of control and tried in vain to stop. Jamie picked up his pace and had managed to get ahead of Sophie, being the quicker runner of the two, *not* as he later tried to explain because he was more scared of the mouse than Sophie!

Up ahead he could see a luminous green square glowing on the wall and decided to stop and see what it was; safe in the knowledge he was far enough away from any little mouse. As his eyes grew accustomed to the glow, he could just make out the emergency escape route instructions.

Before Jamie could do anything about it, Sophie, who hadn't seen Jamie suddenly stop (probably because she had her eyes closed!) collided into him at full speed. Jamie went flying down the corridor slipping and sliding on the recently waxed floor before crashing through Mr Reeve's door. The Headmaster's door!

# Chapter 9 - Mr Reevey's Secret

Jamie came to an abrupt stop, toppling to the ground by a large oak desk which was cluttered with files about finance, marking policies and pupil details. He could see a neat pile of paper clips, a stapler and numerous post-it notes stuck here, there and everywhere, all with illegible handwriting. A collection of mugs, some wishing 'Happy 50th Birthday' and others announcing 'Best Dad' and a host of other bits and bobs crowded the surface of the sturdy desk.

Sophie noticed, as she entered the brightly lit room immediately behind Jamie, that Mr Reeve had one of those eco sensor lights that turn on when someone enters a room and detects when someone leaves. She thought the 'Eco-Warriors' would love this. Sophie peered around the large room with her mouth wide open like it was her first time in this office, which of course wasn't true!

She had to see Mr Reeve last week for hitting Franky Keppel over the head with her brand new pink ruler. She still protests that the ruler slipped out of her bag, into her hand and then just happened to land on the back of his head!

'Wow! I never knew Reevey was 50!' excalimed Sophie in amazement, lifting the large mug, emblazoned with 50, from the table.

'Don't go breaking anything, clumsy, we don't want to get in trouble.' said Jamie irritably as he lifted himself up off the floor.

'Get into any trouble! I don't know how we could get into trouble?' replied Sophie sarcastically. 'Oh, hang on a minute...we stayed in school after it was locked up, we entered Reevey's office and picked through his stuff....no I can't see why we'd get into trouble!'

'All I said was....' Just as Jamie was about to counter argue Sophie, already resigned to losing the argument, he spotted an open drawer at the top of a tall filing cabinet. 'Hey! Reevey's left a drawer open. Let's take a look!'

Jamie rushed past Sophie who, uninterested in the drawer, continued investigating the desk in more detail. He reached the old oak effect filing cabinet and thought it looked like a cheap catalogue job as none of the drawers appeared level.

He tried to pull the drawer but it seemed to be stuck. Not giving up, with the prospect of getting his hands on top secret files, he placed both hands on the handle and pulled with all his might. It didn't budge at first and held firm until Jamie heard something plastic snap.

The drawer flew open with a horrendous screech as the metal runner was gouged by another metal object. Jamie threw up his hands to protect his face and winced, fully expecting the draw to flatten his face. As quickly as it got going it stopped, caught like a fish on a hook, by the metal drawer stoppers.

Jamie peeked through his fingers to see the hard wooden draw front just millimetres from his face. He let out a huge sigh of relief, realising his face had been spared a pummelling and looked over into the drawer. To his huge disappointment all he found were financial records and other stuff to do with maths, not his favourite subject and not the hot gossip that Kate would have loved to get her hands on!

Meanwhile, Sophie was so engrossed in looking through the personal possessions of the Head, she didn't even flinch when Jamie made a pig's ear of opening the drawer. Instead, she was looking at a family photo. It looked like it was taken in Spain or some other hot country, and Sophie could make out a sunburnt Mr Reeve wearing a very bright and colourful shirt which was teamed with khaki shorts. He was standing next to a very beautiful woman. Sophie presumed she must be Mrs Reeve.

Looking closer, Sophie identified two children, the smaller one being his daughter. She had known he had a younger daughter as he had often brought her into school for various productions. She looked like her mum, luckily for her, and had short brown hair, blue eyes and always wore expensive designer clothes. Kate had to look after little Sarah Reeve during Jack and the Beanstalk one

Christmas and told us that even at the age of six she knew the difference between Abercrombie & Fitch and Hollister. The second, taller girl looked around Sophie's age and she wondered why she had never seen her before and observed that she was very pretty.

'Wow, who's the brunette in the bikini!'

Sophie shook her head dissaprovingly. Jamie seemed to have only one thing on his mind! Sophie glimpsed at some writing in the corner of the photo and took a closer look to see if it held any answers. 'I think that's Mr Reeve's daughter. He's written it here in the corner, 'Martha and the girls – family holiday, Spain'.'

'She's a very pretty girl! Luckily, she doesn't take after her dad!'

'Think about it Jamie. If you were to go out with Reevey's daughter, what could happen?'

Sophie gave Jamie time to think it through, although one glance at Jamie, open mouthed with a dazed look on his face, meant she had no chance of getting through to him. She turned the photo over to snap Jamie out of his trance.

‘Just imagine going around her house. Reevey would be checking whether you’d done your homework or he’d try to interrogate you about your grades or how much effort you put in during English lessons!’

Sophie left Jamie pondering whether it would be worth the risk and continued her search around the top of the desk. There wasn’t much of interest, just a few scribbled notes to call different parents, a gold fountain pen inscribed with the words ‘Be swift to hear, slow to speak’ (Sophie thought Kate needed to read that!), a couple of magazines that looked utterly boring and a computer, keyboard and mouse. Sophie knew there was no point in turning on the computer as all the office computers needed a password to gain access.

‘I’ve got an idea!’ Sophie said, excited at her own idea. ‘Let’s pretend you’re the Headteacher and I’m Kate after she was summoned to and see Mr Reeve.’

‘When did Kate have to go to see the Head?’ asked Jamie, rather surprised.

‘Oh my gosh! Didn’t Kate tell you about it last week? Everyone else knows about it.’

'I was ill, remember? With tonsillitis! I only came back to school two days ago.'

'I can't believe Max didn't tell you when you got back!'

'You must have known I was ill. What did Kate do?' asked Jamie.

Sophie ignored the question and continued with her questioning. 'But what about Alfie, surely he would have told you? What about…

'No! No-one told me! Why don't you just tell me!' interrupted Jamie, rather annoyed that he was the last to hear the hot gossip.

'It all happened last Tuesday. Kate was given a Double Dare to kiss Chris Jenkins.'

'Chris Jenkins? But she's wanted to do that for ages. That's not a dare!'

'Yeah, but then she also had to pour the whole of her water bottle over his head.'

'Something she probably *didn't* want to do.' added Jamie.

‘No, you’re right, all attempts to ask him out have failed and this was going to be the end of her endeavours. However, a dare’s a dare and at least she was going to get to kiss him!’

‘A bit of a wet kiss!’ said Jamie

Sophie continued, ignoring the bad joke.

‘Chris was across the field, near the year three classroom, playing tennis up against the wall with Toby. She went to get her water bottle and we all watched as she slowly walked over to where they were, mid-game with Chris 40-30 up. She watched them for about five minutes, which, she told us later, was when she really thought about backing out but took one look at us all watching from the side-lines and she knew she couldn’t. It was quickly coming to the end of lunchtime and she was going to miss her opportunity by just watching. I had to go over and tell her that she had to do it before lunch ended or she would have had to do an Unbreakable Triple Dare!’

‘Oh, so she got dared to kiss someone she liked and I had to wear a dress. Where is the fairness in that?’ interjected Jamie, very sarcastically.

'Look, be quiet and let me finish!' Jamie went back to listening intently to Sophie's story, trying to come to terms with the unfairness of it all. 'Kate knew she had to do it and went straight up to Chris who was in the middle of a forearm smash that nearly took Kate's head off. He immediately went over to apologise to her, not realising what was about to happen to him. As soon as Chris placed his hand on Kate's arm she turned around and planted a kiss on his lips.'

'His what?'

'She just meant to kiss him on the check but totally missed. Chris was stood centimetres away, stunned and bemused just staring at Kate, not really knowing what to say or do. Kate had already taken the lid off her bottle and lifted it behind Chris' back, unbeknown to him. She paused for a brief moment, having second thoughts, but continued to twist her hand, which was now above his head, and sent a waterfall cascading down over his short brown hair, onto his white school shirt which then ran down his grey school trousers making it look like he'd wet himself. His shirt turned instantly translucent, saturated by the amount of water poured over him.' Sophie paused for breath, ensuring Jamie was following it all before she continued.

'As Chris was spluttering and spitting the water from his mouth, Kate made a move to run back to Hugh, not realising that Mr Reeve was standing right behind her. He had seen it all from the year three classroom where he was taking Spanish Club. His face was a picture of rage and when he started to shout the whole school stopped what they were doing and starred at Kate, who was still holding the evidence in her hand. Not a sound could be heard across the school even the birds stopped their merry tune and flew quickly from the scene. Kate was marched into the school where we all prayed she would survive the Reevey interrogation. It wasn't until the end of the day that we saw Kate again. We all charged into the cloakroom, when told to get our bags, to find out what had happened.'

'Did she get away with it?' asked Jamie wanting to know all the details. 'She couldn't have said anything about it being part of a dare or we wouldn't be here tonight! Come on, tell us what she said.'

'Well, you can be Mr Reeve and I'll be Kate and I'll show you how she managed to survive being suspended.' Sophie walked around to the other side of the table.

'Ok.' Jamie went to sit in the comfortable leather office chair that had many levers to adjust the height, back depth, tilting mechanism and swivel. By the time Jamie had played with all of them, nearly falling off at one point, Sophie was standing in front of the desk, crying.

'Why are you crying?' he asked with a concerned tone.

Sophie immediately stopped crying and looked incredulously at Jamie. 'You're not meant to be compassionate, you're meant to be angry. I'm acting if you couldn't tell. Kate started crying when she was stood in front of the desk.'

'Was that part of her plan?' Jamie continued, stepping out of character once more.

'Look, are you going to act like Mr Reeve or not?' Sophie was just about to give up on the whole drama role-play when Jamie slapped his hands hard on the desk, making the photograph and mug lift off the table.

'What have you got to say for yourself young lady? And don't even think about lying to me or you'll find yourself in even more trouble!'

Sophie was quite impressed with Jamie and his believable Mr Reeve impression. She even started thinking about signing him up for the drama club until he spoke again. 'I asked you a question Kate Elizabeth Webb!'

Continuing in character, Sophie replied 'I'm sorry, Mr Reeve. I thought Chris loved me and he didn't! I've also had stomach cramps all day and I can get very emotional very quickly. I'm sorry but I just snapped, he ripped my heart in two and I emptied my bottle of water over his head. Why didn't he love me? '

'Kate asked Reevey that?' Sophie shot him a look that had 'stay in role' written across it. 'Sorry…erm…' there was a pause while Jamie thought of a reply. 'I don't know what to say Sophie.'

'What was I thinking? That you might possibly have a clue what Kate was talking about! Mr Reeve was caught off guard but must have been sympathetic and, as we now know, probably thought of his own daughter growing up and not being able to understand the changes to her body and out of control emotions.'

'So what did he say to her?' questioned Jamie impressed at how accurately Sophie was able to retell the information. He thought Kate must have repeated it many times to many people, just not to him!

'I think for the first time in the recorded history of St Marks, Mr Reeve actually showed he had a caring side. In her best Mr Reeve impression she repeated what he had said. 'It is totally normal to be confused. You're growing up and your body is going through many changes. Maybe Christopher wasn't ready for a relationship yet but I don't think that is any reason to pour water over him. There are better ways to deal with your disappointment. I would like you to apologise to Christopher and then come to me tomorrow during play and lunchtime to reflect on what you did!'

'He let her off with a measly detention? She was very lucky.'

‘Not lucky. A very clever girl! Now I think we should get this office back to normal otherwise Reevey will know we’ve been here!’

Jamie pushed closed the broken drawer hoping that it had always been like that or that the next person to open it would think that they had broken it! Sophie made sure that the photo was placed on the desk at just the right angle and returned the chair to its original position, or as close as she could get it after Jamie’s meddling.

Jamie was about to check that the door hadn’t been broken by their dramatic entrance, when he heard a curious sound coming from outside. He stopped what he was doing and listened carefully but then heard nothing. Thinking it was just his imagination he continued to look carefully at the door handle until he heard the strange sound again.

‘Sophie, stop what you’re doing and listen. I just heard something out in the corridor.’

‘Oh no! Do you think Mr Jones has returned to school early?’

‘No, otherwise the lights in the corridor would be on. Listen it’s not footsteps I heard, it was a sort of…banging.’

They both listened intently waiting expectantly for the next sound. Jamie held his breath to sharpen his listening while Sophie closed her eyes, concentrating hard in the hope of hearing or feeling something.

But nothing!

Not a tremor could be felt.

They both started to relax and even giggled a little, thinking they’d been a bit silly and that it had just been their imagination, when suddenly there was a loud bang! It made every muscle in their bodies contract within a split second, and lifted them both off the ground, the only sound being their sharp intake of breath. They looked at one another, shocked and worried as the echo continued to reverberate around the still and silent school.

# Chapter 10 - Haunted Hall

'What made that sound?' wondered Sophie, as she peered around the wooden door frame of the headmaster's office.

'I don't know. I think it came from the hall. Why don't you go and find out.'

'Why should I go? I thought you were supposed to be the tough one!'

'Oh I see! You don't want to go because you're scared. That's fine! If you don't think you're up to it, being a girl and all.' The last thing Jamie wanted to do was go into a dark empty hall and find out what the noise was. He was tough but he was also scared. Jamie was going to do anything he could to get Sophie to go instead. 'I can't believe Max thought you were different to other girls; more adventurous and brave. I suppose he must have been talking about another girl.'

Sophie took the bait at once, allowing Jamie to feel like an expert fisherman pulling in a huge salmon with a beautifully tied fly.

On cue, her pent-up rage exploded. 'I'll show you what girls can do! I'm going down to the hall right now to show *you* Jamie Matthew Karr!' She turned and walked confidently out through the door, disappearing from Jamie's view and left him, still trembling, standing by the door.

It didn't take Sophie long to reach the hall doors as they weren't far from the Headteacher's office. However, her newly found confidence diminished quickly when she heard the sound, even louder this time, coming from behind the thick wooden doors.

She glanced back along the narrow corridor, floodlit at one end by Mr Reeve's room open door. She could make out the scared silhouette of a boy, hugging the door frame and peering nervously out.

Trembling with fear she continued, knowing only too well that Jamie would tease her if she didn't. She reached out and placed her small shaking hand on the cold door knob and slowly turned it until it clicked open.

The heavy door creaked under its own weight, as it swung it open, revealing an empty hall. The brightly coloured curtains, high up the wall on either side of the windows, were open like a stage awaiting its next act. The moon was lurking backstage, awaiting its entrance behind large dark clouds which were already performing a fast and furious dance across the framed sky. On any normal day Sophie would have been transfixed by the clouds, imagining elaborate (and human-like) shapes, but tonight she could only see vampires and werewolves flying overhead, casting shadows onto the wooden floor below which gave her the creeps.

Every time the moon peeked through the window, the whole hall filled momentarily with an icy cold light which was then suddenly blocked out by passing clouds, returning the room to darkness. This random light show reminded her of the film, 'Alone in the Dark'. She had seen it last Saturday at Holly's sleepover.

Sophie didn't know why they had chosen to watch a scary film as they all hated scary films. And they made it worse for themselves by turning all the lights off and closing all the curtains. Sophie didn't see much of the film as she spent most of it hidden behind her pink feather-filled pillow.

The part she was brave enough to watch was when a young girl was home alone and a storm was raging outside. Her torch kept flickering on and off as she searched for some candles. As lightning flashed outside it lit the whole house up, just as the moon was doing in the school hall.

The little girl had just entered the dark hallway when she heard a knock on the front door. She turned her head towards the single frosted window in the door and saw an outline of a figure. Scared, she ran along the corridor in the opposite direction, towards the safety of the kitchen.

She skidded along the black tiled floor and quickly sat with her back to the fridge. Then another flash of lightning startled her. She saw a dark strange figure looking in at her through the rain splattered kitchen window, its face hidden and dripping from the rain beating down. A bloodied hand was pressed up against the window. It bore scars and had skin peeling off. As it moved from the window and retreated into the darkness, a smudged bloody hand print was left as the only evidence that someone had been there.

All the girls at the sleepover screamed in unison and Sophie and Kate held tightly onto each other, not wanting to watch but intrigued to find out what was going to happen.

Next, the door handle could be seen rattling and then slowly turning until the click of the door, as it opened, could be heard. The girl sat frozen, watching the wind beaten rain splash onto the tiled floor. Holly, at that point, had her hands grasped firmly around Sophie's arm, with her finger nails digging in painfully, breaking the skin.

The shadowy figure stepped into the kitchen with its large muddy boots. They all held their breath in anticipation of a knife being pulled from the nearby knife rack, sitting on the kitchen worktop.

It was absolutely quiet…then suddenly Sophie and the other girls let out a high pitched scream. Connor, Holly's little brother, had run into the room wearing a scary mask Connor who ran, laughing, from the scene.

Sophie and the others never went back to watching the film as they had already had enough frights for one evening and wanted to make sure Connor would regret his devious joke.

It seemed to Sophie that she was now the frightened girl in the film and the constant flashing of light did nothing to alleviate her concerns. She walked in looking for the cause of the banging, hoping it would be easily explained but fearing it could be something not quite of this world or the next.

Her eyes darted over to the four house shields which hung on the wall. She looked carefully at them from Darwin to Einstein, thinking that they might have returned from the dead to haunt the school hall. Not a flinch or even a wink – it couldn't be the pictures. Sophie proceeded to walk to the middle of the enormous vacant hall to get a better look around.

BANG!!

Sophie spun instantly around and saw that the PE cupboard door was ajar and now slightly swaying. Every instinct told Sophie to turn and run but she defied this impulse, taking careful and deliberate steps towards the mystery which lay behind the door.

Her right hand was shaking uncontrollably as she placed her fingers slowly around the edge of the door. She took a deep breath and quickly swung it wide open. Balls of all shapes and sizes tumbled down on top of her, engulfing her like a waterfall crashing to the ground and then rolling and bouncing their way off into the darkness never to be seen again.

Out of the downpour of balls, a few had hit Sophie full in the face, however, she had managed to beat off the lighter balls with a very frantic slapping action and quick footwork.

After the last of the large basketballs had bounced off the side of her face, having broken through Sophie's defences, she looked carefully into the now half empty cupboard for any signs of movement. All she could see in the limited moonlight was a large red bag which was now empty of balls.

'Poltergeists. I knew it!' thought Sophie to herself as she couldn't see any reason for the banging or why the balls would suddenly make a bid for freedom.

BANG!

Once again Sophie pirouetted on the spot and looked at where she thought the sound had come from. She waited for the moon to illuminate the space; the light was not forthcoming and would not reveal the source of the dark and mysterious sound.

As she gazed into the darkness, she thought she could see a snake like creature slithering its way up the wall. It was at least 4m long and the thickness of a drain pipe; it would take two adult hands to completely surround its body. Frozen to the spot, she heard a spine tingling metal echo and the creaking of wood. Sophie's head raced to decipher the species of this strange reptile.

Had she discovered something new? Was it Hogwarts meets St Mark's?

The room then decided to share its secrets, as dark was transformed into light. Sophie saw the truth before her. It was the clattering of a large thick rope striking the metal rungs of the climbing frame after someone had recently finished climbing it. Someone was in the hall!

'J...J...Jamie...is that you?' Sophie hesitantly called out.

There was no answer from the darkness. Her gaze followed the rope up to the high window above and she noticed that it was open. Had someone climbed through the window and down the rope? Where were they now? Had they used the balls as a distraction? Who or what were they after?

Sophie moved away from the cupboard and retraced her steps to the middle of the hall where she tried to view as much of it as possible, whilst light was cast into the hall. She carefully began to rotate on the spot looking intently at the moonlit area.

First to be lit, like an old fashioned slideshow, was the old and out of tune piano, rarely used but wheeled out at Christmas for the traditional infant nativity production. Many at time it stood alongside a young cast member nervously picking his nose or opposite an angel in the front row whose wings had been made by granny and were too big and so poked the children next to her.

Continuing her gaze she looked towards where she thought the school art gallery should be situated, but couldn't pick out any human outline, until the next still picture was revealed. She saw just the weird and ugly Picasso portraits, on the school's art board, made stranger than ever by the moonlight.

Shuffling her feet in a slow arc, Sophie next looked towards an industrial looking structure. Metal poles were welded together topped off with soft looking platforms. Massive wooden 'A' frames of all different sizes were stacked upon each other and reached dizzying heights. A ladder was hung on the wall with large metallic hooks and round and oblong poles all leant together at a jaunty angle. If one fell then they would all follow suit.

Sophie knew this would be a perfect place to hide and approached the structure with trepidation, still unsure of what it was but knowing the next slide would reveal the secrets. Everything went dark and Sophie was left shuffling her feet in the pitch blackness towards imminent danger.

Bright moonlight suddenly revealed the PE equipment, like a magician removing a black cloak. Sophie searched in every nook and cranny but no-one was hiding there and she felt her breathing return to a more regular pace. She quickly felt safer knowing that a knife wielding killer wasn't in the room.

She continued to shuffle around completing a 360 degree sweep of the hall and had closed her eyes and felt relief that it was just her wild imagination that had got the better of her.

As if from nowhere, she felt someone breathing heavily behind her and the hairs on the back of her neck stood to attention once again. She was suddenly frozen to the spot and every muscle began to contract and relax in quick succession causing her body to shake uncontrollably. Her heightened senses listened intently for any sign of a deathly implement being pulled from its harness, like a knife from its sheaf.

All of a sudden, just as she thought things couldn't get worse and that her fate was sealed, she felt a rough hand on her shaking shoulder...

# Chapter 11 - The Stranger

Without a thought of how dangerous her next move could be, Sophie instinctively grasped the hand that had invaded her personal space and, in one swift move, flung the dumbstruck stranger over her shoulder and onto the hard parquet floor. She had only had one Judo lesson to date, but extra practice with Kate's younger brother as the unwilling victim, had meant she was now brilliant at the shoulder throw or Seoi-nage as it was called in her Judo class.

While flying through the air, Sophie managed to turn the helpless body with a flick of her wrist, so that they landed flat on their face. Then as an animal like instinct took over all rational thought, Sophie pounced on the stranger's back and manoeuvred them into a headlock.

'You've messed with the wrong girl, buddy!' spat Sophie as she dug her right knee into the crumpled body beneath her. 'Jamie, help me!' she shouted. The body twisted this way and that like a snake's prey trying one desperate last move to escape. 'Jamie, why are you taking so long? Come and help me!'

'Ugh...I....it..s.....Ugh ge....off....u!' gargled the strangled stranger gasping for his last breath.

'Look, I've warned you once!' Sophie plunged her knee even deeper into his back, trying to cause more pain and to prevent her prey from mounting another attack.

Just as Sophie was about to tighten her grasp around his neck and render him unconscious, she noticed the helpless victim had short dark spikey hair with too much gel on it. Looking more intently she spotted cute little round ears and a bright blue Nike top with a navy blue jumper peeking through.

'Jamie?' The identity of the chocking victim before her slowly began to dawn on her, and she instinctively loosened her grasp.

As she did so, a faint murmur could be heard. 'You....You... nearly killed me! What on earth do you think you were doing?'

Jamie turned over and pushed Sophie off of him roughly. 'If you'd let me speak before going into Judo mode, you would have known it was me!'

'Well, you won't try to sneak up on a girl in the dark again, will you?'

'No way!' replied Jamie rubbing his sore neck. 'Not if all girls are like you!'

Feeling slightly guilty, Sophie held out a hand to help Jamie to his feet. 'I'm sorry.'

Even though Jamie was worried about the possibility of being thrown again, he accepted the peace offering and took hold of Sophie's hand to get up off the floor.

'I can't believe I came rushing into the hall to see what was wrong. You're quite capable of handling things yourself. I'm beginning to think this dare was more trouble than it's worth!' Jamie said, annoyed having got his expensive Nike top dirty from being thrown to the floor.

'Hang on a minute, you can't start thinking of quitting on me. I got triple dared by Holly and I'm not backing out of my dare! Not after all we've been through tonight!'

'What do you mean, we? I'm the one who's been hit, battered and bruised. I haven't seen you get into any trouble. Talk about having it easy!'

'So you don't think being scared out of my wits, thinking an axe murderer was sneaking up behind me is trouble then?

'Look, all I was saying....'

'Yeah, here you go again. Thinking you're the only one with problems. Life always deals you the bad cards. You haven't got a clue what *us* girls have to put up with every month!'

'Oh, *us* boys do. We're clever like that! You don't think I listen during Miss Chalk's Science lessons? Well, I do. Me and Max spent a whole lunchtime discussing how it could affect your mood.'

'You did? You know *all* about it?'

'Yep!' Jamie looked at Sophie smugly. 'New Moon, Waxing Crescent, Half Moon, Waxing Gibbous and then, or course, the *Full Moon*!'

Sophie looked perplexed and didn't have a clue what Jamie was on about.

'Max knew that if the full moon could turn some people into werewolves then it must also have something to do with why you girls are always so moody!'

'Huh! Boys!' Sophie began to wonder if she really would ever understand boys or if they would ever grow up?

Jamie didn't understand the reaction he'd got and put it down to the full moon tonight. 'You were lucky I didn't hit back!'

'Jamie, I am sorry.'

Sophie tried to help Jamie brush himself down until he brushed her hand away, still not forgiving her for what she had just done to him. Sophie thought it was best to step away without saying anything more and let Jamie finish off cleaning himself up.

As Jamie started to re-do his hair, Sophie thought it would be a good opportunity to attempt to build the broken bridge between them.

'I really am sorry Jamie. You've got to believe me.'

Sophie tried to gain eye contact with Jamie to show him she really was sincere in her apology but he averted his eyes, turned away and crossed his arms. Sophie continued in the hope that he was still listening.

'Jamie, we've been friends for a while and you know I wouldn't normally do that to you. It was instinct. I just didn't want to die. I just…' Sophie just didn't know what to say to get a response from Jamie and so decided to sit down quietly on the floor.

The tension in the room grew until it could be cut with a knife and was only punctuated by the banging of the rope against the climbing frame as the wind rattled the wall bars. It felt like hours in the flickering hall before Jamie had calmed down enough to talk to Sophie rationally once more.

'I accept your apology.' whispered Jamie still facing away from Sophie. 'If we're going to get through the night and this dare, we need to stick together.'

Jamie turned around and stuck out his hand as a peace offering just as the hall went dark. Not receiving another hand in return he waved it blindly about hoping to find Sophie's hand. 'Is it a deal?'

'Huh?' It wasn't until the hand was revealed by the light that Sophie could see what Jamie was doing. She picked herself up and took a firm grasp of Jamie's outstretched hand, shaking it. 'Deal!'

'I'm getting hungry. Where do you think we can get some food?' Jamie asked, trying to move on from the assault but the ache around his neck was not letting him forget easily.

# Chapter 12 - Health Free Zone

Sophie knew of only one place that would have food. The room in question was always a mystery to any child at the school. This room was rumoured to have chocolate biscuits, doughnuts, cakes and sweets galore. You were only invited there if you were in trouble or had bumped your head. It was, of course, the staff room!

Sophie took the lead with Jamie walking cautiously behind her, still mindful of recent events. They reached the dark wooden door with a 'Staff Room' label stuck on at eye level and noticed light shining out from a gap beneath the door. Sophie hesitated before slowly opening the door, thinking that they might get caught by one of the teachers.

'Wait Sophie!' whispered Jamie, stopping Sophie in her tracks so that the door slowly closed on them. 'What if Mrs Beach is in there? You've heard the rumours. Alfie told me last week he'd seen the hairs on her legs. What if she's been transformed into a werewolf? It's a full moon tonight!'

'What are you going on about?' Sophie looked at Jamie in disbelief. 'Alfie told me last week that Mr Rogers was a part-time wrestler, just because he has a beard! I didn't think you were that gullible!'

Jamie, now a little flustered, quickly tried to make an excuse, 'No...I'm not...I...was just trying to... scare you! That's all!'

'Oh I thought that's what you were trying to do.' replied Sophie sarcastically. She pushed open the door triggering the eco-friendly light sensor. What could previously only been seen through a small opening in the door, usually blocked by a teacher, could now be seen in full!

The room was quite large and was full with old, worn out chairs, all mismatched and of different styles, placed in two circles, each around a table of a different height. The low coffee table was covered in teaching magazines, birthday collection tins, empty biscuit wrappers and the odd tea mug. It was clear this was where the teachers spent the majority of their time. Jamie tried to imagine all the teachers sitting around at break time, fighting over the last chocolate biscuit and throwing bits of paper at each other across the room. This brought a smile to his face and he couldn't resist sitting in the large leather armchair at the far end of the room, imagining whose it might be and what they might they might talk about whilst in it!

Sophie continued to gaze around the cluttered room. Her eyes fell upon a mountain of books, awaiting marking, topped off with pens of various colours. The source of the light Sophie had seen earlier was the Birdcam laptop.

Mr Ellis had told the whole school during assembly that he had just installed a bird box outside the staffroom and, what's more, a webcam had been fitted so the children could look inside without disturbing the birds. He then went on to explain all about Birdwatch and how the whole school was going to be involved, at which point Sophie had nearly fallen asleep, not being a great bird lover.

She was quickly brought out of her slumber when Mr Ellis began talking excitedly to the entire school about having seen two tits. At this point the whole school erupted into laughter. Sophie even saw teachers biting their lips as they tried to quieten their classes. Immediately realising what he had just said, Mr Ellis corrected himself by saying he had seen two *blue* tits entering the bird box which he thought was very exciting news.

It was a memorable assembly, almost topping the time when the Birdman was invited in to talk about his birds and he let them fly around the hall, only for one of his birds to land on Mr Ward's head, dislodging his toupee!

As Sophie reminisced she continued her self-guided tour of the staffroom. On the walls, timetables, highlighted reports, pins, messages and leaflets were placed under different headings. At one end of the room were lots of pigeon holes filled with paperwork, magazines, payslips and, in Miss Chalk's, she saw a packet of digestives with a half-eaten biscuit lying next to it.

Sophie continued to look around the room and then moved in to look more closely at a very colourful timetable. After a couple of minutes of trying to work out what it was for, she decided the best thing to do was to move on before thoughts of concentrating more during maths lessons took hold.

Jamie, meanwhile, finished his teacher impersonation and walked towards the beech coloured kitchen area, sitting quietly in the corner of the room. ‘Look at this fridge magnet, Sophie,’ laughed Jamie. ‘My idea of a balanced diet is a doughnut in each hand. I bet that’s about Mrs....’

‘Jamie, don’t be so rude!’ snapped Sophie.

Jamie continued to look over one of the tables in the far corner which was covered with piles of books and paper. The first book he picked up had Max’s name on it and was evidently his Maths book. Jamie wondered what comment Miss Chalk had given him, considering he copied most of *his* answers. ‘12th, 17th’ Jamie said to himself as he was flicking through the book reading the dates. '$28^{th}$! There it is. Well done Max! Fantastic work with multiplication and division. I am really pleased with the work you are producing at the moment. 3 House Points.'

Jamie couldn't believe what he was reading as he had done all the work and was quickly rummaging through the rest of the books, to see if he had as many house points as Max.

He was halfway through the pile when he noticed a pale blue folder, normally used by the children to store their worksheets. It had three small letters, S.J.T, inscribed on the top left corner. He considered that S.J.T. might stand for Sophie Jessica Taylor.

He tried tugging at the corner of the folder but it was tightly wedged between some other papers and folders. On top was a heavy yellow folder with Class Profile written across the top, which Jamie picked up before trying to dislodge the mysterious folder.

This time it slid out easily from the mound of brochures, letters and worksheets so that he could see

‘CONFIDENTIAL’ stamped in red letters across the top with a white sticker on the right hand corner giving Sophie’s full name, date of birth and a strange pupil ID number, confirming his initial prediction.

‘Have you found any food yet?’ asked Sophie still looking at one of the easier to understand posters on display.

‘No, but I’ve found a folder with your name on it marked confidential.’

Sophie didn’t register this information immediately and she continued to look at the posters. She then thought about what Jamie had just said and questions ran wildly through her head. Why was her name on a file? Why did a teacher have a file about her? What was confidential about her? Then it slowly dawned on her what was in that file. Jamie couldn’t see in that file. He couldn’t find out what she now knew was in there!

‘Let me have a look.’ Sophie asked, a little too urgently.

'Let me see if it's anything bad and then I can break the news to you gently.' humoured Jamie as he began to open the file to reveal its contents.

Sophie felt her chest tightening and was resolute that Jamie wasn't to discover the contents of the folder.

'Don't open it!' she called out. 'Please!'

'Why? What's in here that you don't want me to see?' Jamie held the folder close to his chest and wrapped both arms protectively around it.

'Jamie please don't open it...I don't want anyone to know!' pleaded Sophie as she raised both her arms in front of her and clasped her hands together as if in prayer.

'Know what, Sophie? Why don't you just tell me or I'll open the file.' Jamie took hold of the folder in one hand again and placed his other hand on the flap of the pocket, taunting Sophie like a doggy treat being held tantalisingly close to a dog's salivating mouth.

'You dare open that file!' shouted Sophie, no longer in prayer, her blood now boiling and sending her into a rage. The transformation from angel to demon took mere seconds and Sophie vaulted the ageing brown armchair in one leap, helped by the adrenalin now flowing through all her veins.

Just as Sophie skirted around the edge of the coffee table, advancing quickly on a startled Jamie, he began to open the file, stopping her in her tracks. Jamie held off opening the folder but stared intently into Sophie's eyes, giving the impression that he was serious about doing it. Sophie, on the other hand, stared back with defeated eyes. 'Ok, I'll tell you, just close the folder!'

Jamie closed the folder, feeling slightly guilty that he had pressured Sophie into telling him. He gripped the file tightly he sat himself down on the wobbly green armchair in front of him. 'Look Sophie, whatever you tell me, I will keep it a secret. You can trust me.'

'Well.....' Sophie thought through all the options, including simply fighting Jamie for it. She decided she had carried the secret long enough and that it was time to share it with someone. 'You know I told you my dad works on the London Stock Exchange for a large American firm and my mum works as a receptionist?' Jamie nodded his head listening intently as Sophie went on. 'Well, that isn't quite the truth, as my dad is unemployed and has had to stack shelves at Price Cutters. Mum does cleaning for a local firm and we have very little money. We couldn't even afford a new uniform this year. I've had to borrow one of Kate's old ones and Mrs Jones gave me her daughters PE kit, as she had outgrown it.'

Jamie's jaw dropped open in disbelief, 'I.....but...you seem...'

'I'm so embarrassed by it all and I didn't want anyone to find out. Kate knows but you can't tell anyone else. In my last school I got bullied because someone found out. The children in my class used to call me a gypsy, a charity case and loads of other horrible things.' Sophie paused, considering whether she should she tell Jamie everything that had happened to her at her old school and would definitely be included in the file.

Sophie had just started back in Year 2 after the Christmas break and was enjoying lunchtime with her friends. A child in her class then approached her and accused her of stealing her little doggie keyring. Because she knew Sophie was poor and was therefore unable to afford one, she jumped to the conclusion that she must have stolen it from her. The girl reported that it had happened while she was in the toilet and accused Sophie during playtime. Sophie denied taking it. (The keyring later turned up in another child's tray!)

The girl went home, still blaming Sophie for stealing her beloved keyring, and told her older sister, who was in Year 6 at the time. She decided that no gypsy girl was going to steal her sister's things and made up a 'Hate Sophie' campaign using her laptop computer.

This involved a display of slides starting which began with a picture of Sophie in school uniform, with her name above it, and then changed to a picture of Sophie's head, edited onto a Victorian street child, dressed in rags and covered in dirt from head to toe. The word 'tramp' flashed above the image and 'thief' below it. The next slide displayed the message: 'If you hate this little gypsy dog and think she should pay then click here.' When you followed the link, it brought up a graph displaying the number of people who had voted 'We Hate Her'.

This spiteful bully then uploaded this presentation onto ViewCube for everyone to see. It received over 3,000 hits during its first hour due to an IM message being sent to every child on the girl's contact list, with a clickable link to the clip. It was like a viral video that spread around the entire web, spreading its cruel, vengeful and untrue message about Sophie.

An anonymous email was sent to Sophie too and, when she clicked on the link, she was horrified and upset to see the pictures and the graph at the end showing that 2,058 people hated her. She read the rest of the email which threatened that if she told anyone about this she would regret it and that they knew where she lived! Sophie was scared and didn't tell her mum or dad about it.

It was the next day at school when Sophie received the insults personally, face to face in the playground. Many children called her the gypsy dog and some children not being so polite! In class, nobody wanted to work with her and during one lesson she was passed a note saying that she should be put down like a dog!

At this point Sophie broke down, crying hysterically in the middle of the class, and when the teacher asked her what was wrong she had the courage to tell her about the children bullying her.

The headteacher, Mrs Woven, was immediately called to the classroom and Sophie repeated tearfully what she had told the class teacher. Her headteacher called Sophie's mum and dad, to tell them what had happened and asked for them to come and take Sophie home.

Mrs Woven then investigated the bullying allegation, questioning lots of children in the process and finding out about the ViewCube clip. She brought up the clip and, on seeing how awful it was, immediately called the Police to find out where it had originated from and ask them to get it blocked, as this was beyond her own technical expertise.

The police took it very seriously and quickly discovered the computers IP address, which had shown who uploaded the clip, and who the registered owner of the computer was. They discovered it was the parents of the Year 6 girl and formally interviewed them at the local police station.

Two police officers came into school to accompany the girl to the police station so that she could be interviewed with her parents. As well as receiving a police caution, which would stay on her record, the girl was expelled from school.

Although the offending hate campaign was instantly removed by the police, Sophie was too scared to return to school and it was months before she was able to set foot out of the house again, for fear of being called names. Sophie's mum and dad decided that they should move and give Sophie a fresh start with a new house and school. So they had all moved to Kent during the summer holidays, ready to start Year 3 in September.

Sophie tried to fight back the tears as the terrible memory resurfaced from the locked vault of her past. She decided that it should stay locked away for ever and continued talking to Jamie, though not revealing the whole truth.

‘I… just…. don’t want that to happen here as I love this school. My friends just...’ Sophie burst into tears, overwhelmed by her emotions, unable to continue talking and collapsed into the nearest seat with her head in her hands.

Jamie felt really awkward. He didn’t have a sister and would usually walk away from girls crying in class. Sophie was really upset; her head still in her hands and her shoulders shaking, and he didn’t know what to do. He felt he needed to show her that he cared and he hadn’t meant to upset her. Jamie walked over to her and placed his hand on her shoulder, trying to show his caring side. ‘It’s okay Sophie, I won’t tell anyone. I promise.’

To Jamie’s complete surprise, Sophie jumped up and hugged him. Their embrace felt to Jamie like it lasted an eternity.

‘Thank you!’ said Sophie as she released her bear hug allowing Jamie to breathe again, wiped away her tears, picked up the packet of biscuits from the pigeon hole and scurried from staffroom as though nothing had happened. ‘Come on, let’s go!’

Jamie, still in shock after being hugged by a girl, decided that what had happened in the staffroom would stay there. He replaced the file carefully where he had found it and put everything back to how it had been, before leaving the staffroom to join Sophie.

# Chapter 13 - Kitchen

It didn't take long for the two famished children to finish off the half packet of digestive biscuits and, as they were both still hungry, they headed towards the school kitchen.

With stomachs rumbling, Sophie and Jamie walked into the darkened corridor where huge fridges and freezers lined each side. It was like walking into a space station miles above the earth. Jamie remembered watching a programme on the Discovery Channel last year. It had stuck in his mind as it was the only educational programme he had willingly sat down to watch. He had seen the astronauts floating weightlessly around a room with very similar equipment, all silver and shiny. If it was one small step for man then it would be one giant leap for Jamie, to ensure he got to the food before Sophie did.

A little way in front, Sophie felt the smooth cold silver door in search of a handle. It didn't take long before she found the industrial sized lever and in one quick movement, pulled open the large door, nearly knocking Jamie over for the second time that night!

'Oops sorry!' said Sophie, holding the open door. 'I didn't know it was going to swing open that much!'

'I'm sure you've got it in for me and just want to find different ways to cause me pain!' replied Jamie, looking at Sophie's illuminated face disappear behind the open door. 'So, is there any food in the fridge?'

If Sophie could have replied, she would have, but she was too busy stuffing chocolate cake into her mouth! However, she thought it a bit strange that she could also taste carrot. It had been sneakily woven into the bottom of the cake, and she though that healthy school status had a lot to answer for as she munched happily on the cake!

Jamie hopped onto the stainless steel worktop as Sophie handed him some fruit yoghurts and an iced cake. He started, as any boy would, on the unhealthiest thing first. However, it wasn't long before he became distracted by a strange buzzing noise followed by a zapping sizzling sound.

He began by looking under the worktop but heard the sound again above him. As Jamie gazed up to the ceiling he noticed a light but it had three blue light tubes instead of the usual white and was creating a mysterious blue glow around the casing. He was transfixed, almost mesmerised by the light and stood up to get a better look.

He continued to move towards the blue glow as if hypnotised. Just as he was about to touch one of the blue bars he heard the buzzing sound again. He turned his head away from the light and saw a black fly winging its way towards him. Jamie followed its path, with his eyes, past his head and hypnotically towards the blue light.

As the fly landed on the blue tube there was a loud ZAP and a small white flash. The fly shook a little and started smoking, then took a nose dive into the tray beneath the light. All Jamie could see was one small helpless fly lying on its back with its leg shaking as if a thousand volts of electricity had just passed through its blackened body. Then the fly was no more!

‘Jamie what on earth are you doing up there?’ Sophie scoffed with half a mouthful of yoghurt spurting out, speckling the shiny clean worktop.

‘I was just staring at this blue light, being drawn in like I was hypnotised and the next thing I know, I’ve just witnessed a fly being murdered by this torture device!’ replied an excited Jamie.

‘Yeah, that is what happens to the flies, they’re attracted to the blue light and then they get electrocuted and die. Which says a lot about the brain size of a fly and yourself!

‘Hey! There you go again, having a go at me.’

‘Well, you do leave yourself open to attack. Try not to do stupid things in the future and I won’t have the need to point them out to you!’ Sophie wiped the yoghurt covered worktop with her sleeve and closed the fridge door, having had enough to eat.

Jamie jumped off the worktop and made his way over to the industrial sized sinks, which were large enough to have a bath in. He looked at the matching stainless steel taps which looked like walking sticks, as they curved over at the top. To the rear of the tap he noticed a snake like hose which was attached at the base and he followed its elongated and coiled body until he found the end. The head was hanging over the edge of the other sink, dripping occasionally down the slippery sides. Jamie picked up the shower-like attachment. 'Look at this Sophie, fancy having your hair washed?'

'Not by you!'

'But look at the size of this thing. I could even have a shower under it!' exclaimed Jamie looking for a way to operate it.

'You remove one piece of clothing and I walk out of here!' Sophie said, covering her eyes in case his thoughts became reality.

'All I wanted was to find out how this thing works but you have to be 'Miss Sensible'. One day…'

'One day you'll what? One day you will do what Jamie?' As Sophie looked at Jamie she noticed he hadn't moved an inch and was holding the shower attachment in his right hand like Poseidon holding his Trident. He was just staring out the window, as if daydreaming. 'Jamie, are you alright?'

'Whatever you do, don't open the fridge again or turn on any lights. I think there's someone on the school field walking this way.' said Jamie, without moving a muscle.

'Look, enough now, I'm not going to fall for any more of your tricks. It was bad enough in the hall and now you're starting again in here.'

'I'm not joking. Come here quickly.' Jamie slowly lowered his shower head and crouched down so he could just see over the top of the window ledge. 'I definitely saw something moving out there on the field.'

Sophie, hearing the seriousness in his voice, quickly ran and crouched down beside him. They both scanned the large open field for anything out of the ordinary. With little light it was difficult to see anything at all, until a definite shadow of a person could be seen moving towards them. Sophie gripped Jamie's arm and they both quickly ducked down, hoping that they hadn't been seen.

Hearts beating quickly and adrenalin flowing through their veins, they couldn't hold back the fear they both felt. Was it the caretaker? Why wasn't he using the front door? Was it a horrible burglar? Would they get hurt?

The realisation that they could soon be in a lot of trouble was overwhelming for Sophie and she began to cry. Jamie, having experienced this before, felt more comfortable about what he had to do next.

He caringly placed his arm around Sophie, comforting her and telling her everything was going to be ok.

'Jamie…I don't want…to be here anymore. I've had enough of this dare.'

Sophie buried her head into Jamie's shoulder and continued to cry. Jamie began to stroke Sophie's hair, like his mum used to do to him when he was scared at night or had grazed his knee. It seemed to work as Sophie soon stopped crying although she continued to hold on to him tightly.

'I've had enough too, Sophie.' Jamie reassuringly whispered into Sophie's ear. 'It was an adventure to begin with but it's not fun anymore.'

Jamie turned Sophie around so she was looking straight at him, he wiped her tears from her face and said 'Come on, let's go home.'

Jamie helped Sophie to her feet and they began to walk past the ovens and low level cupboards moving closer to the fire exit. Sophie briefly turned her head towards the window and saw, through her ghostly reflection that the shadowy figure was now at the end of the building and was running quickly towards them. Then she spotted another figure, following closely behind.

'They're coming Jamie!'

'*They're*? You mean there's more than one. Come on, quickly, through the fire door!'

Jamie rushed to the door on his left and pushed the wide metal bar, releasing the locks at the top and bottom, allowing the brisk night air to rush in which sent a chill down Jamie's spine.

'Wait Jamie! You'll run straight into them if you go that way!' cried Sophie, still looking out of the window at the figures moving quickly towards them and the door.

Jamie was like a confused dog running this way and that, not knowing whether he should risk making a run for it or stay with Sophie and search for another way out.

'Quickly come here!' whispered Sophie as loud as she dared to. 'I can see them coming up the path.'

Jamie released the door and sprinted over to Sophie, but the fire door hadn't closed properly and was left ajar. 'Jamie you've left the door open! You need to close it!'

Jamie skidded to a halt and quickly turned on his heels. He ran towards the door in an attempt to close it before they could enter, but then he saw the door open. Jamie flung himself to the right, between two rows of cabinets, barrel rolling like a commando out of sight. Sophie had already hidden herself behind another unit and was crawling along the floor to join Jamie at the other end of the kitchen.

Two pairs of footsteps could be heard stopping at the other side of the counter and then there was talking in hushed voices, too low for Jamie or Sophie to work out what they were saying or even if they were male or female. They both then heard what sounded like someone taking something out of a rucksack, followed by a click and then a bright torch light lit up the sinks and began to scan the room from left to right like a prison search light. Shortly after this they saw a second bright circle as another torch was switched on and joined in the search.

Jamie tried to slow his breathing as he was sure they could hear the rampaging elephant inside his chest announcing his presence just a few metres from them. He thought that whatever was going to happen wasn't going to be good for either of them. If it was Mr Jones coming back to lock the school and he found them, they could kiss their chances of getting into grammar school goodbye and then look forward to being expelled from St Mark's – the first children this would ever happen to.

Then he considered the possibility that they might be thieves who had entered the building hoping to steal the brand new computers in the ICT suite. If this were the case, they wouldn't take too kindly to anyone seeing who they were. Jamie cringed at the thought of being hit with a baseball bat. Neither outcome looked promising to Jamie.

# Chapter 14 - Intruders

Sophie was sitting on the cold hard floor thinking of all the excuses she could give. 'We got locked in the cupboard and couldn't get out. We tried to call out but no-one could hear us!' was the first one that came to mind. If it was burglars, she was just going to hide and pray!

'We need to get out of here quickly.' Jamie whispered to Sophie who had both hands clasped together deep in prayer. 'I think I know of a way out. Just follow me and don't make a sound.'

Sophie finishing two 'Hail Mary's' and one 'Our Father' and then nodded and followed Jamie as he crawled quietly to the end of the storage unit.

Upon reaching the end of the unit, Jamie held up his hand and clenched his fist. Sophie bumped straight into him. 'That signal means stop!' Jamie whispered in annoyance, demonstrating his clenched fist again.

Sophie then observed a very strange sign language whereby Jamie held two fingers together and then waved them at Sophie and then off to the side like he was directing traffic. He continued to point to himself and then thumbed for a lift.

He repeated this absurd routine a few more times before he became frustrated at the look of confusion spreading across Sophie's face. He whispered in Sophie's ear that she should go right and he'll go to the left. On his signal they should run for the door.

'Why didn't you just say that in the beginning instead of all this finger waving?' Sophie whispered imitating Jamie's hand movements back to him like a bad signer for the deaf. 'I've never played soldiers before!'

Sophie crawled off to the right on all fours leaving Jamie peering around the edge of the unit, quickly pulling back as the light shone his way. He needed some way of distracting the two torch holders away from the fire exit otherwise there would be no means of escape.

Jamie felt around the floor and cabinet edges and luckily came across a screw that had come loose from one of the shelves above. Although not the largest screw in the world, it would do the job.

Taking another quick look around the edge, Jamie glanced across to the wall opposite him and saw a huge stainless steel cube suspended in the air with a large metal bar surrounding it. Underneath was an empty stacking basket and to the right, three full baskets stacked with clean dinner trays. It dawned on Jamie that he was looking at the kitchen's dishwasher and that if he could get his screw to hit the box at the top, it would make a great distraction.

With the screw between his thumb and forefinger, he tossed the screw towards the large metal box, hitting it directly on the side making it ring out like an old church bell. Both beams of light honed in on the location of the sound and footsteps followed, as the pair moved closer. Jamie's plan had worked.

Jamie quietly slid along to the other end, away from the advancing investigators, while Sophie moved forward to the next row of units. He had just reached the end of the row when the footsteps stopped level with him. The beam from one of the torches suddenly changed direction and began searching along the row Jamie was in.

In the nick of time he had managed to scoot around the end of the unit, out of the path of the oncoming light. Jamie was scrunched up as tight as a ball, in the shadow of the cabinet, making sure no part of him or his clothing was caught in the searchlight now sweeping from left to right. If they had decided to walk along the row, moving the torch a centimetre to the left, it would have easily illuminated his bright blue top and  the game would then be up!

Uninterested in an empty row, the light reverted to searching the dishwasher and its surrounding area. Jamie peaked over the top of the unit and found his view was blocked by a metal colander, which prompted his second idea.

He slowly reached out across the shiny worktop and placed his hand around the large meshed bowl. With a quick flick of his arm, the colander slid across the shiny surface and flew off the edge, hitting the lunch hall shutters and causing an ear splitting crash before falling to the floor and rolling around.

The enormous crash had the desired effect. The torch lights instantly sought the site of the object, which tumbled around like a fifty pence piece being spun on a table.

While the two strangers were distracted, Jamie, in one swift move, leaped up and over the closest worktop to the exit and shouted 'Noooowwwww!'

'Is that the signal?' asked Sophie as she stood up and started to run towards the door as quickly as her weary legs would carry her.

'Sophie? Jamie? Is that you?'

Jamie and Sophie, recognising the familiar voice, stopped in their tracks, although neither quite understood why they were hearing it.

Both torches homed in on their faces, blinding them as though it was an interrogation. Holding her arm up in front of her face trying to make out who was holding the torch, Sophie called out. 'Kate, is that you?'

'Oh bum, my torch has gone out!' said another familiar voice.

'Yes it's me, Sophie, and my *pain* of a brother. Here Johnny, give me that torch! I knew I shouldn't have let you hold it!'

Kate grabbed the broken torch from her brother and pointed her own torch to the ground, allowing Jamie and Sophie's eyes to become accustomed to the semi-darkness.

'Sorry we startled you. I thought you'd seen us and opened the door for us.'

'We thought you were burglars!' exclaimed Sophie, as she ran up and gave Kate the biggest hug of her life. 'I'm so you're not!'

'I'm glad we're not too. You might have decided to hit us with something instead of running!'

'So why are you here?' asked Jamie.

'The others decided, as my garden backs onto the school field, I should jump over and see if you two were still in school, completing your dare. My brother caught me leaving the house and said he'd scream if I didn't take him with me. So here he is too.'

A little 5 year old boy wearing action man pyjamas, sheepishly waved at Sophie and Jamie before running to hide behind Kate. 'Little brothers! Who'd have them? So what've you two been up to?

Jamie and Sophie looked at each other and both said 'Nothing much!'

# Chapter 15 - It's All Gone Pink

Sophie embraced Kate once more while Jamie tried to fix Johnny's torch. It wasn't long before the brief moment of calm was cut short as all the lights suddenly turned on, as if by magic.

'It's the caretaker! He's back to lock up.' said Jamie, running to the kitchen door, leading out towards the hall. He looked through the small round window shaped like a porthole and noticed that the lights were on in the hall as well. He could now see that the parquet floor was littered with different sized balls. 'It won't take him long to lock up all the classrooms, check the hall, the staffroom and then find us here in the kitchen. We'd better get out of here!'

'Quick, follow me.' said Kate taking hold of Johnny and pushing him out of the fire door.

They all ran across the damp field up to the fence that led to Kate's garden. Johnny quickly found the fifth wooden panel, moved it to one side and slid through the gap into his garden. The other three quickly followed and Kate then swung the broken panel back into place as if it was new again.

'Thank you, Kate. You saved our lives.' said Sophie, giving Kate another hug. Jamie was also very thankful but felt he had had enough hugging for one evening!

Kate led the way along the dimly lit path past a huge empty mobile home, back up to the house. She lived in a large detached house that her dad had just recently renovated. It had taken him over a year to finish the work and during that time she had had to live in the small mobile home, perched on the back garden lawn, sharing a room with her brothers, which she hated. It felt like the worst year of Kate's life as she couldn't have friends to stay overnight, and opted to spend most nights over at Sophie's. During the winter months she was bitterly cold and resorted to wearing extra layers of clothing to try and stay warm.

It took such a long time to complete as Kate's dad was now a builder, after his short-lived pop career hadn't earned him enough money, and so he could only work on the house in the evenings and during weekends. Kate loved being with her dad whenever he was working on the house and knew all about knocking down walls and building them up again, plumbing in sinks and showers and also how to plaster walls.

What she looked forward to the most was if she had any free time during the weekends and her dad wasn't working on the house. Kate would set up her acoustic electric guitar, amp and microphone in the empty shell that was to be her room and sing her favourite songs to her heart's content. The acoustics in the room were brilliant and only amplified her amazing voice! She felt like she was at a large concert hall playing to thousands of fans who had come to see her (especially as her younger brother had been in the room and drawn lots of pictures of people on the partition wall using his big crayons). It's where she had practised for the Talent Show seven nights in a row! It meant she also didn't have to worry about annoying anyone else as her parents left her to it and she was all alone in the half-built house.

‘So where are your parents tonight Kate?’ asked Jamie, worried that her parents wouldn’t take too kindly to him turning up in the middle of the night.

‘It’s their wedding anniversary today and they decided to celebrate by going to see Keith Bowlan, an ex-band member who hit the big time. He’s playing at the O2 Arena. Afterwards they’re having dinner and staying overnight at a really posh hotel. Debbie, our babysitter, is looking after us and she’s brought her annoying boyfriend over. They’ll probably be too busy making out on the sofa to notice anyone else coming or going. They probably wouldn’t even notice an earthquake!

Kate noticed that Sophie was looking worried as she glanced over towards where the curtains were shut and all the lights were turned off.

‘Don’t worry, Sophie. Your parents haven’t called once while you were gone. They think you’ve been here all night.’

Sophie felt a huge weight lift off her shoulders and she began to relax, knowing she wasn't going to be grounded by her parents.

Kate opened the back kitchen door and turned to her little brother, squatting down to his eye level. 'If you say anything at all to anyone about tonight, I'll tell Mum that you were the one that broke her Lladro figures and not the cat!'

Johnny immediately understood the trouble he could be in after he had destroyed his Mum's precious figure while playing football in the newly decorated living room, just after the house had been completed.

He had been strictly forbidden to play any ball games in the lavishly styled room but wanted more room to practice his penalty kicks. The hallway was too narrow to practice his Beckham style free kicks.

He had set up the goal with the two arms of the sofa being posts and the penalty spot being positioned between the two single seat settees. The crowd were going wild: the tall giraffe which had been brought back from a trip to Africa, and was usually to be found by the hallway door; his and his older brother Ben's Action Men along with some Barbies from Kate's room. He knew he shouldn't have gone into Kate's room but the crowd was looking a little sparse for his liking. He had set the toys up against the fire place and was pleased with how it resembled Wembley Stadium, with his Mum's precious Lladro figures positioned on the upper terrace.

Their mum had just popped over to see Gill, their next door neighbour and Sophie's mum, to pick up Kate who had stayed overnight with Sophie. Johnny knew he didn't have long to score the winning goal.

George the Gorilla was sitting on the centre of the goal line getting ready to make the winning save. Johnny took three steps back and the crowd went silent. He took one step forward, and then another, and then struck the ball so that it hit the top left hand corner of the imaginary goal post and scored an amazing goal. George was left stranded on his goal line, not even moving as the ball shot past him.

Johnny was mid-way through his celebration when the ball ricocheted off the window and was sent flying towards the ornate mantelpiece. It was as if he was watching a slow motion replay of 'What happened next'!

The ball skimmed past the sitting ballerina and knocked into the little boy wearing a polo top, looking adoringly at his faithful Labrador companion by his side. The force of the ball allowed it to slide to the edge of the mantelpiece but then it stopped briefly before toppling over the edge.

Frozen to the spot, Johnny watched as the ball continue to bounce along the mantelpiece, heading towards an expensive porcelain piece called 'Butterfly Treasures' – a long brown haired girl wearing a long flowing dress with pretty pink and blue flowers near the hem. She carried a basket with small delicate butterflies fluttering around it. Johnny's dad had bought it while on holiday in Spain for his mum's 40th birthday.

The ball hit the figure square on the chest and sent her toppling over the edge, where she smashed into millions of pieces on the hearth of the fireplace. His golden goal had suddenly turned into his worst nightmare!

Kate had returned to the house before their mum, and saw the devastation in the living room and found her brother crying, frantically trying to clear up the mess and hide it under the sofa.

Johnny, seeing Kate, ran up to her and begged her to help him clear up before their mum returned. He said he didn't want to be grounded and would do anything if Kate would help him.

Kate quickly sped out the door and returned a few minutes later with Spike the cat. She quickly picked up the ball and threw it out into the garden through the patio doors and told her brother to take all the toys by the fireplace to his room.

Kate went to find her mum and told her that the cat had got into the living room and had tried to walk across the mantelpiece, knocking over one of her figures and breaking it.

Their mum was upset for a few days and the cat was banished to the mobile home for a few nights. Their dad, when he found out, quickly logged onto the Lladro website and bought an identical figurine to cheer his wife up, which luckily arrived a few days later. No-one ever found out it was Kate's brother and now it was time for him to return the favour!

Johnny nodded his head and, without a word, went up to bed.

'Sophie you know the way to my room. You can change into some of my spare PJs if you'd like, they're in the first cupboard on the right.'

Sophie walked quietly past the living room noticing that Debbie was already sucking the life out of some unfortunate boy whom she had in a vice-like grip on the sofa, completely oblivious to the film on the TV.

'Come on Jamie. I'll show you the way.' whispered Kate.

She slowly walked through the country style kitchen with exposed brick work and out into the oak hallway. Sophie was already at the top of the stairs and ran into Kate's room to get changed and ready for bed.

Kate turned around to face Jamie, put her finger up to her lips and crept past the living room door. Jamie noticed too, as he got to the open door, that the babysitter was attached at the lips to a boy and running her hands through his wavy hair.

He stopped in the middle of the doorway gawping at the two loved up wrestlers, until Kate pulled him out of view of the babysitter's victim and they both quietly crept up the stairs.

Kate knocked on her bedroom door, 'Hey Sophie, are you changed yet?'

'Yes, you can come in.' Sophie replied.

Kate and Jamie walked into a very sophisticated pink room! I don't think Jamie had ever seen so many pink things in one place before. The walls were covered in a very pale matt pink, with polka dots on top in a slightly darker semi-gloss pink that made the circles stand out.

Looking around the room, he read the words painted on the wall, which he presumed were adjectives describing Kate - caring, loving, beautiful, loyal and trusting. She had pictures of all her friends in little heart shaped frames hanging from her cupboard door. Next to that was a full length mirror inset with even more hearts.

On her dressing table he saw make-up of all colours, hair brushes, pink hair straighteners and a diary. Jamie wondered what might be written about him in the diary and whether it would positive. At least he knew that he would definitely fill a couple of pages after telling Kate all about their dare.

As his eyes continued around the room he noticed Sophie lying on the top bunk of the black metal bunk bed. She was wearing a pink top and bottoms to match the duvet on the bed.

'Jamie, I might have something for you to wear.'

As Kate said this she saw Jamie's horrified face, looking around at all the pink and imagining what he was going to be given to wear. She added quickly to put Jamie at ease. 'Oh, it's alright, don't worry. I'll go to my older brother's room and pull out a spare pair of his PJs!'

Kate pulled out her spare hidden mattress from under the bottom bunk and left the room to fetch Jamie some pyjamas.

Sophie, who had now climbed down to the bottom bunk of the bed, started to question Jamie.

'I can't believe what we've been through this evening! But if we're going to tell Kate everything that happened tonight, you must remember the promise you made in the staff room.'

'Yeah, I remember! But if Kate knows everything already, why can't we tell her?'

'She only knows that my Dad lost his job and I needed to borrow her uniform as we couldn't afford a new one until pay day. She doesn't know how bad things actually are!' Sophie's eyes began to water and she hid her face from Jamie behind the magazine she was reading.

'Look, a promise is a promise, Sophie. Just don't get upset again.'

'Who's upset? I just have something in my eye!'

Jamie decided not to argue with Sophie as he knew how much it meant to her. Sophie quickly changed the topic of conversation. 'So what does your mum think you're doing tonight?

'Well, I've been staying with my dad this week and was supposed to be going to Mum's tonight. So when I asked if I could stay over at Max's tonight, Dad had to call Mum. Luckily the conversation stayed polite as normally they'd start arguing and Mum refuses anything that Dad's asking for. On this occasion she must have been in a good mood, probably because she had Rob, her new boyfriend, staying over and said I could stay at Max's. I hate it when my parents argue!'

'Have your parents been divorced for long?' asked Sophie.

'They split up when I was in Year four but they had been arguing for years before that. I could hear them when I was supposed to be in bed asleep. Dad would come home after being in the pub and it would start off quietly and then the arguing would start. I tried to bury my head in my pillow and block it all out until I fell asleep. Some nights I heard mum running up the stairs crying and then I'd hear Dad opening another can of drink. The next morning you wouldn't know anything was wrong as they put on an act, thinking I hadn't heard them arguing the night before. When Mum and Dad told me they were splitting up, I just felt relief. I could sleep knowing that there wouldn't be any arguing.' Jamie hadn't revealed that to anyone before but felt remarkably comfortable telling Sophie, who was giving Jamie her full attention having put her magazine down. Something had changed between them; he felt closer to Sophie and trusted her completely.

'Of course the arguing didn't stop and after Dad had moved out they started fighting over who should pay the bills and the cost of school trips and who they though should have the silver Audi TT. Mum won that battle, which I was very happy about. Then they'd argue over me and how many days I would stay with Dad. They never asked me what I wanted!'

'So, do they still argue now?'

'Yes, but it's not as bad as it used to be. Dad doesn't like Mum's new boyfriend so they argue about that more than anything else. Dad tries to question me about Rob, whenever I stay with him. I like Rob but I try to say as little as I can about him to Dad or I know he would go off on one of his rants!'

It all went quiet after Jamie stopped talking until Kate returned from Mike's room with some pyjamas for him to put on, even though they were a bit too large for him. She directed him to Mike's room, just one door down, where he could get changed as Mike was staying over at a friend's house that night.

'So, what were you both talking about while I was gone?'

'Oh not much, I was just asking Jamie where his mum thought he was staying. Will your parents be okay about us both staying over?'

'Oh they'll be fine. I asked them before they left if I could have you and some other friends over to stay and they said it would be fine.' said Kate.

'Why did you ask them if you weren't going to have anyone over?'

'Well I did say to you that if there were any problems during your dare you could stay at my mine, so I was just making sure everything was in place in case you didn't stay all night. Also, if your mum spoke to my mum, your cover story wouldn't be blown.'

'Good thinking Kate and I'm glad you did as we had a terrifying night!'

'Come on then, tell me...

Kate was interrupted by Jamie entering the bedroom. Both girls giggled as they looked at Jamie swamped by the oversized striped pyjamas hanging from his slim body. Jamie had rolled up the sleeves so his hands could be seen and left the pyjama bottoms gathered around his feet like wrinkled elephant's feet!'

'Hey, stop that! It's all Kate had.' said Jamie, trying to put an end to the giggling.

'Sorry!' Both girls replied but continued to giggle.

'Sophie was just about to tell me all about what happened to you both.' said Kate as she sat herself down on her pink fluffy bean bag while Jamie sat down on the mattress on the floor.

Sophie and Jamie recounted everything in detail to Kate, except the secrets from the staff room. It was gone midnight by the time they had finished answering all of

Kate's questions as she searched to find out as much gossip as possible, before deciding that they must go to bed and get some sleep as they still had school tomorrow.

Kate climbed up to the top bunk and snuggled into her rose covered duvet, waiting for the other two to settle down before turning the light out. Sophie climbed wearily into the bottom bunk and got under a matching duvet while Jamie had to sleep under Kate's old Barbie duvet.

'Are you all as snug as a bug?' Kate called out.

Both Sophie and Jamie said that she could turn out the light.

After a few minutes in the darkness, Sophie turned to face Jamie, who was lying on the mattress next to the bunk bed and listened to see if Kate was asleep. As she heard Kate sleep talking she knew it was safe to speak to Jamie.

'Jamie, are you awake?'

'Yes,' replied a sleepy Jamie.

'Thanks for keeping my secret.' whispered Sophie.

'That's okay. Do you think we'll get in to trouble tomorrow?'

‘I hope not. I don’t think the caretaker will know we’ve been there.’

There was a slight pause as both thought back over the past few hours.

‘I was really scared tonight, Sophie!’

‘Me too.’

‘Good night Sophie.’

‘Good night, Jamie!’

The events of the day had quickly caught up with both of them and they were soon fast asleep. They knew the inquisition wasn’t over as the rest of the group would want to know all about their adventure. But one thing was certain - they weren’t going to take risks again. Well, not until the next dare!

## The End

Lightning Source UK Ltd.
Milton Keynes UK
05 January 2011

165199UK00001B/26/P

*CS00122302TRP*